THE SPIDER:
THE CORPSE CARGO

THE

MASTER OF MEN!

SPIDER®

THE CORPSE CARGO

By Grant Stockbridge

ALTUS PRESS • 2019

CHAPTER 1
A MYSTERIOUS SUMMONS

R ICHARD WENTWORTH'S hands were light on the steering wheel, his eyes warily sharp as he searched the night blackness of Clark Street. The summons to visit the Police Commissioner's home had been casual, but there had been an undercurrent of tension in Kirkpatrick's quiet words, of tension and—fear!

Wentworth clicked off all lights and let his sleek roadster drift with only the faint whisper of the engine, the purr of its fat tires, to betray its passage. At the far corner of the next block, fronting on Hardesty Boulevard, the Commissioner's home sat remotely amid wide-spread grounds. But Wentworth had no intention of entering the gates openly. A single vertical line creased his smooth brows as he recalled Stanley Kirkpatrick's clipped, precise words.

"Dick," Kirkpatrick had said over the phone, "could you drop over to my home at once? Yes, my home. And, Dick, if you could come—" there had been a pause of seconds there, "if you could come... unobtrusively... it would be better for us both."

Kirkpatrick had refused further information over the phone, and this secrecy was not like the Police Commissioner. Nor did that accent of fear fit into his character. There was some dark mystery here, else why should the Spider be summoned—secretly—to the Commissioner's home?

1

THE SPIDER

The train pirates struck. Green-white flame spurted like
jabbed forked lightning from the train.

Wentworth caught up a silver-headed cane from the seat and stepped from the car to the narrow foot pavement along Clark Street. An untrimmed ten-foot hedge, backed by a stone wall, crowded close. He walked quietly toward a certain familiar break in that hedge, where a quick vault would put him inside Kirkpatrick's grounds, "unobtrusively."

He frowned slightly as he located the break he sought, then his firm, mobile lips curved into a slight smile. Unless his eyes played him false—and the Spider's eyes were incredibly keen—a

3

man had moved in that black opening in the hedge. That meant just one thing. Kirkpatrick's home was watched!

When he was still twenty-five feet from the break, other shoes than his own made small rasping noises on the pavement, and a man stepped slowly and deliberately into his path. Wentworth continued his unhurried stroll, muscles relaxed. The man's heavy, short body was silhouetted faintly against the dim rays of the corner street light. His head was thrust forward, shoulders hunched. But he waited quietly until Wentworth had covered fifteen feet, and then he spoke:

"Got a match, Buddy?"

Wentworth's smile tugged at his mouth corners again as he strolled to within a single stride of the man. An old trick, this. Either a man, reaching for a match, dipped his right hand into his pocket and was hampered when the attack was made; or, if the intent was less violent, he revealed his face in the glimmer.

Wentworth slid his left hand to his vest pocket. He gripped his cane lightly in his right fist, knob uppermost. The solid silver knob was round and heavy.

"I have no matches," he said casually, "but I can give you a light."

HE SLIPPED out a small cigarette lighter whose platinum sides glinted dully, and snapped it into flame, the cane poised and ready in his right hand. A bulbous face moved into the halo-glow, a face of sagging jowls with a rosy, button nose. The man wheezed as he sucked in smoke. His eyes sought Wentworth's face across the yellow cone of flame.

But Wentworth held the lighter so the shadow of his fist fell

4

blackly across his countenance. When the man's cigarette glowed, he snapped out the lighter. The man straightened with apparent reluctance, hesitated, then mumbled his thanks and moved to pass.

Wentworth stepped aside politely, turned to walk on. His straining ears caught the sharp rasp of gritty shoe leather. He ducked and whirled, as a swishing blackjack missed his head by an inch!

The fat man grunted in surprise. Wentworth snapped his right arm upward and the silver cane head clicked against his assailant's jaw. The man's breath hissed out and he went down hard.

Wentworth peered swiftly up and down Clark Street. It was deserted. Swiftly he bent over the man and ran through his pockets, found papers identifying him as Ralph Donaghue of the Black Detective Agency.

A low whistle hissed between Wentworth's teeth as he jerked erect. Why were private detectives watching the Police Commissioner's home? But there was no time for speculation now. He must move fast. There was, it seemed, work for the Spider!

His eyes were withdrawn and alert as he was ushered ceremoniously into Kirkpatrick's home office, but there was a warm smile on his vital, clean-cut face.

Kirkpatrick rose behind his desk, a faultlessly attired man a trifle taller than Wentworth's scant six feet. His long, saturnine face was smiling slightly, moving the waxed points of a neat mustache.

He shook Wentworth's hand. "You've thinned up some, Dick," he said casually.

Wentworth smiled at him blandly. For the present, he wouldn't mention that encounter in the dark. Better to learn first the reason for this summons, the reason the Commissioner of Police called in such a notorious criminal as the Spider. Replying to Kirkpatrick's mention of his thinner, paler face, he reminded him of the recent weeks he had spent in the hospital recovering from wounds.* He limped slightly, favoring his left leg, as he moved toward a chair a suavely waved hand indicated. He sat back and continued to smile, but his eyes were questioning.

He and Kirkpatrick were warm friends, drawn together by mutual admiration and respect. But between them was a barrier, the insurmountable barrier of the law!

On one side was Richard Wentworth, whom the world knew as a wealthy clubman who sometimes gave charity concerts, playing a violin that sang with the soul of genius, or who, again, brought back some rare beast, alive, from the wilds of far Sumatra, or purchased some fabulously valuable painting. They

---

* Author's Note: I remember Richard Wentworth's weeks in the hospital as some of the happiest days of his life. His fiancée, Nita Van Sloan, was constantly at his side and despite the pain of his wounds, suffered in his conflict with the man he dubbed "the Devil"—I recounted that adventure in the story called "Satan's Death Blast"—he was gay and an almost normal being. But he was ever impatient for action and despite the felicity of having Nita at his side—a thing rarely possible in his life of constant perils—he had left the hospital at least a week ahead of schedule.

knew him for a great philanthropist given to freakish, but sociologically sound, benefices. But of his real altruism as the Spider only a trusted few knew. For that mysterious avenger who brought his swift and awful justice to the Underworld was a criminal and a murderer in the eyes of the law!

Kirkpatrick had long ago become convinced that Wentworth was the Spider, but because of his intense admiration for the man, because Wentworth administered swift justice where Kirkpatrick's law-hampered forces could not act, he had declared an armed truce. If Kirkpatrick ever found positive proof that Wentworth was the Spider, he had sworn to act with the full power of his office. But until such time as the proof should fall into Kirkpatrick's hands, he would assist Wentworth in every way possible. And the Spider would return the favor.

"Why this mysterious night call?" Wentworth asked.

KIRKPATRICK, SEATED now behind his desk, glanced toward the drawn window shades, toward the closed door, and then dipped two fingers into a vest pocket. He held across the desk a signet ring on whose seal a sprawling, hairy-legged figure glowed crimson. And as he held the thing his hand trembled slightly. Wentworth's smile did not alter. No tension crept into his body. Yet the thing he gazed upon was his own signet ring, and on it had been imprinted *the seal of the Spider!*

Kirkpatrick was talking hurriedly, half fearfully, his eyes sharp upon Wentworth's lean face.

"There is no need for fencing between us, Dick," he said in his quick, clipped accent. "You and I both know you are the Spider, but I'm not trying to trap you. I think this ring brings some sort of message to you and I am afraid to think what that message is.

"I asked you to come secretly because I wish no one to know that I have this ring, or that I know what to do with such a ring when it comes into my hands."

Wentworth asked: "Where did you get that ring?"

His thoughts raced back over months of battle against the Underworld. He knew when last he had worn that ring. It had been a simple signet then, but he had printed his seal upon it and given it to a boy of twelve who had helped save the Spider's life.* He had told that boy: "If you ever need help, send this ring to Stanley Kirkpatrick, Commissioner of Police, and I will come."

Now young Jim Walsh must need the Spider's help! But

---

* AUTHOR'S NOTE: I related this adventure of Richard Wentworth in the story called "Citadel of Hell." Wentworth had been trapped, half dead from fatigue and nearly overcome by smoke in a burning warehouse. The boy, whose brothers and mother Wentworth had saved from a fire led a fireman to where Wentworth lay. Afterward, when the fireman discovered a fire bomb an enemy had planted upon him, the boy stirred up a mob to attempt to lynch Wentworth and thus, by diverting the attention of the police, permitted him to break away and escape. The plan was a product of the Spider's fertile brain, but the boy executed his part of the arrangement so well that Wentworth felt he owed him his life. He gave the boy the ring as a talisman in case of trouble, knowing that if the ring came into Kirkpatrick's hands, Wentworth would be sure to learn about it.

what of that detective on watch outside the house? Surely he was not connected with the boy!

Wentworth leaned forward tensely. "Quickly, Kirk," he said. "This is important. Where did you get that ring?"

Kirkpatrick's saturnine face was grave.

"A boy came here," he said, "and insisted on seeing me. He gave me this ring and seemed to think I would know what to do with it. He refused absolutely to say anything except to give his name and address."

Kirkpatrick took a slip of paper from his drawer. "James Walsh," he read, "723 Dugan Street."

Wentworth snapped, "Thanks!" and reached the door in two strides.

"Wait, Dick," Kirkpatrick cried.

The door closed. Wentworth caught his hat from the expressionless butler and went long-legged to his car. When he spun the corner the detective he had knocked out had disappeared. **THOUGHTS CROWDED** thickly as Wentworth raced southward through the city. He was sure that young Jim Walsh would not have sought help for himself. Time and again Wentworth's secret charities had tried to help the boy and his family, only to meet self-reliant refusal. No, there was more to this than a call for help—though the Spider would gladly have answered such an appeal. Jim Walsh had uncovered some new threat to society. The detective's attack lent support to that....

The streets grew narrow and twisting. Tenements reared their squalid brick walls to either side, their slatternly fire escapes draped with the poor people who panted for relief from the heat. The streets were like ovens and hot wind fanned his face. Children, too listless to play, sat soddenly on the blistering curbstones. The air was heavy and rancid with the smells of close-packed humanity. In the sweltering heart of this district, Dugan Street writhed its crooked way.

Around the corner from Dugan Street, Wentworth parked his car and pushed on afoot, cane swinging, his slight limp hardly perceptible. The heat of the pavements penetrated his shoe soles. He paused by a tenement wall to light a cigarette, and the brick radiated warmth like an oven. The platinum side of his lighter made a perfect mirror. In it he surveyed the street, but found no pursuer.

He slipped the lighter into his pocket and hurried on. He reached the Walsh home and, pausing a moment in the black shadows, fastened on a blond mustache and wig, placed small bits of hard rubber so that they distended his lips and altered his nose. It was a crude disguise, but in the dim light it would pass.

He climbed to the boy's home on the third floor of a tenement. At his knock, Mrs. Walsh, a heavy woman, her unkempt hair stringy with perspiration, her broad face good-humored, opened the door. She held a baby straddling her hip and laughed at Wentworth's request for Jim.

"Sure, and Jim is over in the shack with his Spider club," she said, indicating its direction with a jerk of her thumb. "And is the spalpeen the popular member of the family these days!"

"I don't getcha," Wentworth said with a Bowery accent.

The woman kept on chuckling. "You're the second man to come asking after me boy tonight," she said, "and…."

She gaped at empty darkness. A moment before a man with a blond mustache had stood there. Now, a shadow moved swiftly down the steps.

Descending with long, rapid strides, Wentworth was grim-faced and fearful. If another man had asked for Jim tonight, the Spider might already be too late! For that query could mean but one thing. The menace Jim feared, the threat he sought to expose to the Spider, was closing in upon him.

Past a sputtering gas jet, Wentworth whirled back along the first-floor hall. Mrs. Walsh had pointed this way when she mentioned Jim's "shack." He guessed that by "shack," she meant a shanty such as boys out of time immemorial have erected from scrap wood for their "secret club" meetings.

Wentworth legged out into the night, spotted instantly a huddle of blackness in the middle of the vacant rear lot from which a gleam of light escaped. That would be the shack. He raced toward it.

Then, abruptly, Wentworth flung flat down on his face on the hot dusty earth. A bullet whined past his head. He had seen the glint of warning metal a half second before. But there came now no flash of powder flame and no crash of gunfire. A silenced revolver!

Wentworth lay unmoving, scanning the shadows with keen, hard eyes. A silenced gun spelled organized crime! Nothing less! Jim Walsh had done well to send for the Spider. Heaven grant that the Spider's coming was not too late!

11

CHAPTER 2
THE TORTURE KNIFE

WENTWORTH'S HEART-BEATS quickened—but not through fear. The shot had undoubtedly been fired by a lookout. That meant, undoubtedly, that he was in time!

He flashed a look over his shoulder and saw then what had betrayed him. A pale gleam of light from the sputtering gas jet of the hall had outlined him as he plunged from the back door. He would again be visible to that hidden marksman if he attempted to regain his feet. His lips drew back from his white teeth in a tight smile.

He held only his cane, gripped by its tip so that its solid silver head dangled, as he got to his feet and soundlessly continued his advance. Useless to probe the shadows to either side of the shanty. They were impenetrable. His only hope was that the gunman guard would go to that door which showed a thin line of light, go there to warn them that a man had dashed from the tenement where Jim Walsh lived, and that that man had vanished at a shot.

And then Wentworth saw a shadow move.

It made a vertical black bar across the line of light beneath the shanty door, the shadow of a man's leg. Wentworth whirled the cane once around his head and let fly. On swift, silent feet he raced after its hissing flight.

He heard it thud soddenly and clatter softly in the dust. He sprinted hard and caught the man he had struck before his falling body could strike the ground and alarm those within the shack. He eased the man down, ran sensitive fingers over his head. There was a deep depression where the cane had struck. The throat was pulseless. A gangster had paid for a shot in the dark.

Withdrawing the man's silenced gun, Wentworth crouched against the shack's door, ear to the crack.

Through that crack came a sound that chilled Wentworth's blood, that bared his teeth in blazing fury. It was the choked cry of a child in terrible pain, a whimpering, muffled moan of agony! There filtered out also an odor that made his stomach turn over with nausea, that sent his hands flying to his guns. *Good God!* That odor was the stench of *burning human flesh!*

Wentworth jerked erect and, a gun in each hand, kicked open the door. It smashed loose from its hinges, slammed down flat with a violent crash. The flame of a single candle on a box jumped and went out, but the shanty was still filled with ghastly light, a green-white glare that flickered gruesomely over the crouched figures in the room.

The green glow came from a knife in the hand of a man who crouched over a supine boy. Sparks glittered and danced along that six-inch blade and turned green the terrified glances of six boys, painted hideously the three men who held them at gun point.

These things Wentworth saw at a glance, then the silenced revolver in his right hand began speaking with its soft, deadly voice. Four bullets sped, then Wentworth sprang inside. The ghastly green glare of the knife died and he snatched out his pocket flashlight, dropping the empty revolver, and waited tensely with his automatic ready.

The man who had crouched over the prostrate boy with the green-glittering knife had pitched backward to the floor with a bullet hole in his forehead. Another shot had driven the second man back against the wall, and as Wentworth watched, he slid slowly down upon his heels. His feet popped out straight and he slumped over sideways and did not move.

The third man had taken the lead between his shoulders. He had held a gun in either hand, trained on the captive boys, but those hands were hanging limply at his sides now as he dropped in a contorted huddle.

WENTWORTH CROSSED swiftly to the door and raised it into place. He whisked his small light's ray over the startled boy faces about him.

"It's all right," he said, forcing cheerfulness into his voice. "It's all right. I am the Spider."

He lighted the lone candle again and dropped down on his knees beside the boy who lay on his back on the floor. The eyes were shut and a gag of wire and wood had torn his mouth. The clothing had been ripped from the scrawny child's chest and Wentworth shuddered at what had been done to the white flesh.

He fought the gag from between the boy's jaws and touched his throat. No pulse. He forced himself then to inspect the wound in the boy's chest. On the bared flesh had been burned with slow torturing heat a flag with a skull and crossbones upon it. The mouth of the death's head was not burned. It was a deep knife thrust, but it had not bled.

Wentworth reached for the knife torturer. His weapon of torment was clenched in his dead hand and Wentworth tore it loose, inspecting it with loathing. A wrench pulled hilt from blade and revealed a small battery and a tiny transformer of strange design.

Wentworth stared at the implement blankly. In heaven's name, how could so tiny a battery create the heat to inflict those fearful wounds? How could it generate an electric discharge that would light the entire room? His fine lips tightened into a grimace of horror as he realized the potency of this thing.

The Underworld had seized another weapon against humanity. This knife alone was a fearful weapon, but the principle embodied here, the ability to step infinitesimal power into gigantic force, threatened unspeakable crimes!

His muscles tight with fury, Wentworth stood staring down at the torturer's dead body, clenching the parts of the knife. Gradually he forced himself to calm. He stepped across the small shanty to the back wall. A banner hung there, a black banner upon which unskilled hands had fashioned an awkward spider in crimson. Wentworth took that banner down and laid it reverently over the body of the boy who had died. He turned to the others then.

"Where is Jim Walsh?" he asked.

No one answered, and Wentworth forced himself to be calm.

Anger had edged his voice, anger for the horror that had been wrought here. Slowly his body relaxed from its tense fury. A wan smile touched his lips. He picked out a boy with dark, tousled hair and a swarthy face.

"Giorgio," he said quietly, "where *is* Jim?"

The boy shook his head jerkily. "Dunno," he said.

"Do you know why he wanted me to come here?" Wentworth asked again.

Suddenly the boy began to stutter out words, half Italian, half English.

"Jim just told us to meet here tonight," he said rapidly. "He say he go and get you and then he tell us all what it's about. But Jim not come back yet and these men come and tie up Jack…." Horror stopped his voice and his eyes flickered toward the dead boy on the floor.

Wentworth snuffed out the candle. "You boys all go outside and wait for me and then we'll have a little talk."

In the darkness, he stooped over the bodies of the men he had killed, the three who lay within and the one who lay without, and he touched the forehead of each with the base of his cigarette lighter…. When the police came, the wide beams of their flashlights would glisten on a crimson spot on the forehead of each man to show who had made them pay for their brutal crime, to warn the Underworld of swift vengeance to come—*the sprawling sinister seal of the Spider!*

Then Wentworth gathered the huddled boys about him and walked toward the tenement house. They sat on the back stoop in the half-darkness that the gas jet behind only faintly illumined.

"Now tell me, Giorgio," he said softly.

THE BOY'S voice began faintly, choked by tears, but gradually became firmer. After Jim Walsh had helped the Spider, and been given the Spider's own gold signet ring, Jim had banded the boys of the neighborhood in a secret club. They had secret signs and deemed themselves the Spider's assistants. Watching the chronicle of his crusades in the newspapers, they had tried to find things to do for him. And this afternoon, excitedly, Jim Walsh had called them together and told them he was going to call the Spider. That was all he knew.

The dead boy was Jack Curley, who lived with his grandfather over on Bentley Street. His grandfather was an inventor.

Wentworth seized on those words, jerking to his feet. An inventor! The gangsters had tortured his grandson and with a device that surely was the work of some electrical genius! This, then, was the secret behind the attack. Once more the brutal hand of the Underworld was reaching out for a weapon to attack civilization. It had reached into the home of this hidden genius for that weapon, and torture and death had followed. There lay the answer to this summons from young Walsh. But where was the boy?

"Listen, boys," Wentworth said. "It is a great thing to help the law, and the police. Keep doing that. But the work of the Spider is not for you. You must never involve yourself in anything like this again. Go to the policeman on your beat and tell him you want to help enforce the law and he will tell you what you can do. Keep your club if you like and work with it, but I would never sleep again if you came to harm through me. Go home now and tell your parents what has happened."

He darted to the street, jerked the swift roadster into speed, racing to the home of the boy who had been killed. That way lay the trail. He must pick it up there, thwart these criminals and rescue Jim Walsh. A grim sense of defeat tugged at Wentworth's heart. He alone, he felt, was responsible for that boy's horrible death.

Wentworth swung into Bentley Street, skidded to a halt and ran to the house where the slain boy had lived. He took the steps two at a time. Curley lived on the top floor, the boys had said. As Wentworth passed the third floor, he twisted out the gas jet and whirled into the next flight to find darkness above, too.

That darkness was ominous. Had the torturers come here, too? Slow foot after slow soundless foot, he pressed up the stairway, his cane questing, feeling out the darkness ahead.

Wentworth felt it touch something that yielded and he jabbed viciously. A man grunted in pain, and the light of an electric torch fanned into Wentworth's face!

"Don't move," the man's voice rasped. "Don't move, or I'll drill you."

CHAPTER 3
GREEN FIRE OF DEATH

THE MAN was beyond the thrust of his cane's tip, but the hand torch—that, at least, was within easy reach.

Wentworth snapped the ferrule upward. It clicked against metal and the beam of light jerked to the ceiling.

The man cursed. His gun lanced flame. But Wentworth had flung aside and jerked erect. Even as the shot crashed, he sprang to the landing, and struck upward fiercely with the knob of his cane. It crunched bone and the torch shattered on the floor. The man's body thumped down, and a door to the left flung open, slashing the darkness with a wide oblong of light. It silhouetted a crouching man who gripped a gun.

"Cracker!" he cried, a frightened question in his voice.

Wentworth straightened out his body in a savage swordsman's lunge with the cane's tip. The man's gun arm caught the direct force of the thrust and the weapon flew wide. Even as it clattered to the floor, the man sprang forward, steel gleaming in his left hand. Wentworth shrank aside from his charge, heard his feet stumble, then beat swiftly down the steps.

Another figure stood in the doorway now, the bent-shouldered thin figure of an old man. Behind him a woman's blonde head showed.

"What's going on here?" the old man demanded in a firm voice.

"Are you Jack Curley's grandfather?" Wentworth snapped from the shadows.

"Yes, I'm Jack Curley's grandfather," the old man admitted, uncertainty creeping into his firm voice. "What's the matter?"

"Get out of here and register at the Hubert Hotel," Wentworth told him swiftly. "Here's money. It's a matter of life and death!"

19

He tossed money to the old man and raced down the stairs behind the fleeing gunman. He burst out into the street in time to see an open car whirl a corner with whining tires. Wentworth sprang to his roadster and had it around that same corner before the other car had swung from sight again. He trailed it for several blocks, then parked his car and caught a taxi.

The driver of the fleeing car, apparently satisfied he had shaken off pursuit, stopped his twisting and doubling and sped northward, weaving swiftly through thinning traffic. The car, its top down, was a Packard phaeton, and speedy. It took the northbound drive through Central Park and on into Lexington Avenue at a smooth forty miles an hour.

An hour later it was droning along the Bronx River Parkway, Wentworth's taxi still stubbornly on his trail. There was no doubt now that the gangs were after the aged inventor. Wentworth was positive that he had averted some serious threat there. But what was even more important, he had picked up a hot trail that he hoped would lead him to the headquarters of the gang and enable him to rescue young Jim Walsh, for whose apparent capture he bitterly blamed himself.

Wentworth smiled mirthlessly, watching the bobbing red taillight ahead. He turned to inspect the black stretch of road behind, felt his heart jerk once, then flung to his knees on the floor. A heavy car, coming fast and without lights, was no more than fifty feet behind! Even as Wentworth snatched out his automatic, the car began to pull alongside.

Wentworth leveled his gun and waited. The cab driver jerked his head about and the taxi wobbled crazily.

A man thrust his head out of the other car. Wentworth drew a bead on him, waiting for the glint he was sure would herald the death cackle of a machine gun.

"Pull over!" yelled the man. "We're cops!"

THE TAXI shuddered to a weaving halt, the other car pacing it, and the man who had leaned from the window climbed out.

As he approached, the taxi's lights illuminated a heavily jowled face, a rosy, button nose. It was the private detective Wentworth had felled near Kirkpatrick's home!

"Sorry to bother you, buddy," the detective said, "but I'm a cop and I got to get back to town. I've got to get help for my buddies in that other car." He yelled at the driver, "Back to town."

Wentworth slipped out his gun and dug its muzzle into the detective's fat side. He found and removed the man's gun.

"Sorry to contradict you," he said gently. "Driver, go straight ahead."

The taxi man twisted a small, angry face toward them.

"Listen," he snarled, "youse guys make up your minds, see?"

Wentworth leveled a second gun at the driver.

"Follow that car ahead," he directed.

The driver gaped at the gun, at the fat, surprised face of the detective, then whirled and sent the car lurching forward.

"Look here," the detective remonstrated, "I'm a private dick, see, Donaghue of the Black Agency. You'll get in trouble for interfering with me this way."

Wentworth laughed softly, pocketed the gun he had leveled

"JIM" WALSH

JONAS CURLEY

at the taxi driver and shook a cigarette clear of a case, stuck it on his lip.

"How does your jaw feel?" he asked solicitously. He watched the detective's face swing toward him and offered him a cigarette. "I have no matches, but I can give you a light."

He snapped the yellow cone of flame to his lighter and in its circle of radiance, studied the startled button eyes beside the button nose. The small, puckered mouth was wide open.

"BOLO"

"CAPTAIN KIDD"

"Geez!" gulped the detective. "You're the guy what beaned me up in Clark street. I'll get you for that!"

"A tough dick, eh?" Wentworth laughed mockingly. He pocketed the lighter and his voice got thin. "Listen, louse, who hired you to slug me tonight?"

"Go to hell," said Donaghue.

Wentworth gouged the gun harder into his fat side.

"Don't," gasped Donaghue. "That hurts."

"Who hired you to follow me tonight?"

The detective half whimpered. "I don't know. Honest to God, I don't. The Chief just tells me to trail a certain kid, see? I do that and then my partner takes the kid and I'm to follow the next guy that comes to that big house the kid visited. I see you coast up without lights so I try to take you. That's all I know about it, honest."

Wentworth's eyes were narrow in the darkness, surveying the hulk of the detective beside him. The man was scared and his words had the ring of sincerity.

"What do you mean, your partner took the kid?" he demanded.

He could read surprise in the man's answer.

"Why, he followed him is all."

"Okay," Wentworth said. "Driver, stop here."

The cabbie braked down and Wentworth shoved the detective out. The man ducked and ran zigzag up the road, diving into the nearest shrubbery.

"Drive on," Wentworth said. "And don't lose that car ahead."

WENTWORTH WAS frowning through his grim amusement over the private dick's flight. Still, all was mystery. He had found no explanation of why the gangsters had attacked, nor of their weird and horrible torture. No explanation of that Pirate's flag that had been burned on Jack Curley's chest. And now a carload of private detectives was on the trail as well!

"Slow," he barked sharply at the driver. He had spotted the dark blur of the detectives' unlighted car whirling into a side road.

"Turn off your lights," he ordered.

In complete darkness, feeling the way over a road that made the taxi jounce squeakily, Wentworth continued the pursuit. They bumped over a double-track railway crossing where a light glittered like a green eye, pushed on, climbing steeply with thick trees close.

"Stop the cab," he said, and, when the man obeyed, "Get out and hoof it," he ordered.

"It's my cab," the man whined. "You wouldn't take away a poor man's—"

Wentworth cursed impatiently and the man flinched away. The drone of the other car's engine, climbing in second gear, was fading.

Wentworth thrust money into his hand, far more than the cab was worth. He got behind the wheel and sent the taxi surging through the darkness. He topped the hill, started a wild, jouncing descent.

Suddenly, without warning, the night ahead was aflame with a ghastly glare. Green and white fire sheeted the road ahead. Wentworth jabbed at the brakes, saw the detectives' car black against a livid glare of light, saw green and white sparks dancing over its framework. Then utter blackness shut down.

He heard the car ahead crash like a shelf of crockery dumped to the floor. Then silence added itself to the sudden darkness, and on all that road ahead there seemed no stir of life.

Wentworth yanked on the emergency and spilled from the cab while it still rolled. He recognized that green fire. It was the same that had glittered along that fiendish torture knife! He sprinted down the road until he was within feet of where the car had wrecked amid green-white flames. Then he moved cautiously. He drew a pencil torch and threw its thin beam along the road, located the smashed car and hurried toward it.

The darkness and silence about him were absolute. There wasn't even a groan from the victims of the wreck. Wentworth peered into the car. Four bodies were contorted in there, tragically motionless. He touched the car cautiously with the tip of his finger, jerked it away. The metal was blistering hot and the smell of scorched enamel was thick on the air. Scorched paint and another nauseous odor that once before tonight had made his blood run cold. The odor of burning human flesh!

Wentworth used his hat as a pad and twisted open the front door of the car, hauled the driver out and laid him on the ground. He was dead and an inspection showed his shoe soles were burned. The palm of his right hand held the searing mark of hot iron. But none of those could kill. Abruptly, Wentworth understood and the knowledge jerked him erect, left him staring unbelievingly down at that dead body.

The man had been electrocuted, killed by a terrific electric current while he drove openly along a dark country road, killed by the Green Fire! Fire? Good lord, *it was chained lightning!*

Nothing of less intensity than a lightning bolt—and that meant millions of volts!—could bathe a speeding car in such green-white flame, scorch it with superheat and kill the men—all in a space of less than the time of a heart beat.

Slowly the trembling left his body. He stood stiffly, hands clenched into white fists. No wonder criminals had tortured and slain to grasp this powerful weapon! No wonder they had seized this work of electrical genius from its inventor! Once more the Underworld had struck horribly at civilization. Death was here in awful form, death inflicted by a weapon which in criminal hands could rock the entire world!

CHAPTER 4
TRAIL OF DEATH

WENTWORTH SEARCHED the roadsides and found two stiff lengths of wire which projected to the road from a fence post on one side and a telephone pole on the other. The wires failed to meet by about three feet. Obviously, these wires had carried that terrific charge of electricity and the car's metal nose had gone into the gap between them and had caused the short circuit and the blast of the Green Fire.

Grimly, he traced the wires and found both tied into the telephone cables. Telephone wires, he knew, carried no such powerful current. It was apparent that somewhere the gangsters had led their enormously stepped-up voltage—this current must multiply amperage, too, to kill so swiftly!—into these cables. If he found that spot, he might easily run to earth the inhuman fiends behind this atrocity; he might ward off this threat to human life and society!

He raced back to the taxi and ran it into the cover of nearby trees, then began tracing the telephone wires. The ground was hard under his feet and grass rustled dryly with his tread. It was after midnight and at last the earth's surface had thrown off the heat of the day. Wentworth made rapid headway along the wires. He ran from pole to pole, stopping at each to send the pencil ray of his light questing upward. Finding no lead-out wire, he raced on to the next.

For a mile, two miles he pushed on like that. Perspiration dampened his hair, wilted his stiff collar. His shirt clung to his back. Another mile and the wires cut off from the road and went striding on long-legged stilts across the fields.

Suddenly, without warning, a half dozen electric torches flung their white beams at him from all sides! Wentworth's hand darted to his gun, but he realized at once the futility of resistance. From the elder thicket ahead, from the thick-growing broom straw to right and left, the lights blazed and guns glinted. Behind him, he heard feet pound the earth then suck into mud. Metal gouged into his back.

"Lift 'em, buddy," a cold voice ordered.

Wentworth's futile investigation of many poles had dulled his alertness and he had walked squarely into a trap. His feet were ankle deep in mud, hampering quick movement. He might knock out one or two lights, but more than that would be impossible. And there still would be four lights, four men with ready guns. He lifted his hands slowly.

"What the hell is this?" he demanded indignantly. "Can't a guy walk across a field and…."

"Not this field, buddy," the voice behind him said.

A hand patted over his pockets, found and removed two guns and the pressure of the hard knob in his back increased.

"Straight ahead," the man ordered.

WENTWORTH PEERED up beneath the sagging brim

of his hat. They were climbing steadily now, and in the glimmer of starlight, he made out the dark loom of nearby buildings. The rustle of feet in the broom straw ended and shoes clumped on hard-packed earth, trooped up to a bulky house, through a narrow door and into a room lighted only by the hand torches.

The two men ahead, silhouetted against the reflected light, were visible now. Both were small and quick-moving, One of them bent and lifted a trap door.

A shaft of light gushed upward. Still covered by many guns, Wentworth went down open steps slowly, blinking to accustom his eyes to the brilliant light.

Four more men were seated around a wooden table. They held cards in their hands and all looked fixedly at Wentworth. The cellar smelt of stale beer and tobacco smoke. The smoke eddied upward until the trap door was closed.

The man spoke from behind him.

"Tell the chief I want to report," he said.

One of the men at the table, a boy with a weakly good-looking face, got up and sauntered toward the far side of the cellar. Wentworth saw roseate light when the door opened there. He frowned and twisted about to confront the man behind him. The fellow was emaciated, a half head taller than Wentworth's own five feet eleven. The man grinned and thin lips slid back from buck teeth.

"Well, buddy, how do you like it?" he asked.

Wentworth surveyed him from head to muddy feet.

"Lousy," he said. "Just another lousy bum."

He turned his back on the man's cursing and the others

laughed. The slight, good-looking boy returned and jerked his head backward toward the low door of roseate light.

"Go on in, Bill," he said, "and bring what you got along with you."

The knob of the gun muzzle jabbed violently into Wentworth's back. He walked curiously toward the door, ducked his head to

"I dislike having to move, Bill," she said gently. At the final
word she lifted her automatic and fired once.

go through. There was only one gun covering him now, the one
held against his back. When he ducked to enter, that, too, pulled
away.

Wentworth pivoted completely on his heel and slammed his fist upward just as the man called Bill ducked his greater height through the door. Bill's head bumped the low ceiling and Wentworth hit him again, knocked him clear of the opening and kicked the door shut.

He heard Bill's gun hit the floor inside the room and he dived for it on his belly.

"Just stay like that," a voice ordered, and Wentworth twisted his head about and saw a woman with a leveled gun.

BILL'S WEAPON was still lost in the dimness of a remote corner and Wentworth got slowly to his feet. The woman was smiling slightly, standing beside a luxurious davenport over which a floor lamp hooded roseate light. She was dressed in a soft yellow gown with long sleeves and a very low neck. Her hair was black and crisp and cut close like a man's. It gave her small, dark face piquancy and would have made her charming except for the eyes. Her eyes were heavy lidded and venomous as a snake's.

"That was rather silly of you," she said, with a suggestion of a lisp.

Wentworth stood without speaking, eyes swiftly scanning over the room. It was decked out with every luxury. There was a single door beside the one he had closed.

"My bedroom," said the woman.

She sank languidly on the davenport, holding the gun in her left hand on the arm of the davenport. With her right hand she reached out and pulled an indolent cat into her lap. It had long white hair and bright blue eyes and stared at Wentworth unwinkingly.

"My bedroom," the woman went on, lingering over the words, "but it has only this one door and no windows. That's why you were silly to knock out Bill."

As she mentioned his name, the lanky man on the floor moaned and tossed an angular arm across his face. The woman turned her intent, heavy-lidded eyes toward him and watched until he heaved himself to his feet. He stared about him blearily, spied Wentworth and pounded toward him.

The woman said, "Don't, Bill."

She said it gently, but the man stopped as if transfixed with a knife.

"You had something to report, I believe," she asked.

Bill still glowered at Wentworth but at the woman's words, he swung his head toward her.

"I got plenty," he said. "Them four guys that went to find out who the Curley kid was squealing to...."

"I got information on the kid from other sources," the woman said shortly. "I'm not in the least interested in their failures."

"Failures!" Bill grunted. "Hell! Them four was bumped!"

The woman's searing curses interrupted him. It was not mere blasphemy. It was blistering obscenity and when she pronounced the words, her lips writhed like two small red snakes.

"You ain't heard nothing yet," said Bill gloomily. "It was the Spider what done it."

"The Spider!" the woman gasped the words. "But I understood that young Curley got in touch with Kirkpatrick through the

Walsh kid!" She was staring fixedly at Bill, and Wentworth edged forward, moving his feet by invisible fractions of an inch.

"I knew the Spider would cut in on the game sooner or later," she went on heavily, spitting out another stream of profanity, "but I'll be damned if I thought he'd do it so quickly. What else?"

"Well," Bill began, "Cracker and me was up at old Curley's place throwing a scare into the old man so he wouldn't blab about his granddaughter being snatched…."

A thought like a flash of light brushed Wentworth's mind. He had the explanation of the whole thing! These gangsters had kidnaped Curley's granddaughter and held her hostage to prevent the old man from revealing the theft of his transformer. That was why, fearing harm to the captive if police were told, the Walsh boy had taken the Spider's ring to Kirkpatrick. And young Curley had paid with his life for talking….

BILL WAS still talking: "Some bozo barged in on the party me and Cracker was holding with the old man… Jeez, Chief, that daughter of old man Curley is some good-looker!"

That, Wentworth thought, would be the blonde he had seen over Jonas Curley's shoulder.

"Get on with the story," the woman said drily.

"Well, it's like I was telling you," Bill continued. "This bozo barges in and conks Cracker. I lights out for here with that bozo still on my tail. I shook him and somewhere I picked up a load of private dicks." A slow, ugly grin began to twist his face. "I ran into some of the other boys by the plant down the road—

that's where I got the dope about the Spider—and we burned out the dicks."

"I was waiting for that," said the woman gently.

Bill's words choked off and he stared at her and his eyes got wide. He licked his lips.

"For gawd-sake," he gulped, "the plant was put there to use, wasn't it?"

"Go on with the story," said the woman.

"Well," Bill said slowly, "after that we hangs around to see whether anything else will happen and after a while we see a guy walking along the telephone poles flashing his light up each one of them. He didn't find out nothing. We waited for him and brought him along. This here is the guy."

The woman turned her slow, heavy eyes on Wentworth.

"Why were you flashing your light on those poles?" she asked quietly.

Wentworth smiled at her. He had advanced two full feet toward the davenport. "I was looking for my cat," he said. "I always take my cat riding with me and sometimes she gets away. Agatha has such a fondness for telephone poles, you see."

The woman smiled with her lips that were like fed snakes.

"And do you always wear a false mustache and a wig when you hunt your cat?" she asked. "Take them off him, Bill."

Bill did that violently, taking some skin along with it. Wentworth made no resistance. His time would come later....

"Now, tie up the gentleman, Bill," the woman ordered.

He did that, too, with the same vicious thoroughness. When

Wentworth lay trussed like a chicken upon the floor, the woman spoke softly.

"Bill," she called, and, her voice was caressing.

Bill was bending over. He jerked his head sideways to stare at the woman.

"Bill," said the woman, "that neat little trick of yours in burning out those detectives is going to make it necessary to move."

Bill straightened, hands pleading.

"For gawd-sake, Chief," he said, "we either had to do that, or—"

His words choked in his throat as the woman spoke again.

"I dislike having to move, Bill," she said gently. She lifted the automatic from the cushioned arm of the davenport and fired once. Bill started a hoarse cry, his pleading hands thrust out stiffly before him. His head jerked up and his back arched. His knees gave first and he crumpled in an angular heap on the soft golden pile of the rug.

The door from the outer cellar flung open and two men jammed through. The woman looked at them lazily from beneath her heavy lids.

"Take out this carrion before it messes up the rug," she ordered.

CHAPTER 5
THE MURDER QUEEN

THE TWO men stood unmoving in the doorway for a moment, then came forward slowly into the room of roseate light. Wentworth was watching the face of the woman with alert eyes. He flicked a glance at the two men creeping toward the body of their companion like mice stealing into the presence of a hungry cat.

"Hurry, darlings," said the woman sibilantly, "or mama might get angry."

The men sprang at the corpse of Bill and yanked it across the floor to the door.

"Come back, Jack," the woman ordered, and one of the men halted trembling by the door. He turned and inched back. He tried to smile, tried nonchalantly to touch the blond mustache that shadowed his upper lip.

"It's all right, Jack," said the woman. "I just want to give you some further orders."

As the man came to a stand before her, she gestured with the automatic. He flinched, but she was only pointing toward Wentworth.

"Put him with the rest," she said, "and take the old man to the place I told you about. I don't want to see him."

The man's face was questioning. Wentworth watched him narrowly. Whom could the woman mean by the "old man?"

"We've got to move out of here permanently within a half hour," she said, and her voice rasped. "That fool Bill used the

37

emergency plant down the road to burn out four private dicks. We'll have the police down around our ears by morning."

A startled oath escaped Jack and he went toward the door with short, quick strides. The woman turned her sleepy, venomous eyes upon Wentworth. She pushed the cat aside and sauntered toward him.

"It's a pity you can't be more friendly, Spider," she murmured.

Wentworth stared up at her fixedly. He recognized that he was in the presence of a criminal genius of utter ruthlessness. She held her gangsters in a grip of mortal terror. Heaven only knew how the woman had learned his identity, but he could see she spoke from definite knowledge. It was not a bluff. He smiled up at her blandly.

"You flatter me," he said.

She nodded her head at him. "I expected to have an accounting with you before we finished with this affair, but you acted too quickly for me. And now that I have seen you, I know the only accounting that will be satisfactory is—" she smiled lazily, "—your death!"

The door opened again and Jack and the other man caught up Wentworth. The two men lugged him across the other cellar room into a small dark bin where they dumped him on the floor. Before Wentworth could loosen his bonds they came back a second time and carted him upstairs into what apparently had been the living room of the house.

The woman stood there and the last piece of her furniture, the heavy davenport, was being carted out into the night by five straining men. At her orders, two men unbound and stripped

Wentworth to the skin while she calmly held a pistol upon him. They found the tool kit which Wentworth carried always strapped beneath his arm and which contained many deft instruments which he had devised for his work. Then his arms and legs were bound again and he was made fast to an iron ring in the wall.

He knew it would take hours to get free. Hours, and this woman planned to kill him. He knew already her murderous efficiency. He would be lucky if he had even minutes to escape! THE WOMAN smiled at him slowly, apparently reading his thoughts. She held the automatic carelessly pointed at his breast, as the men went below stairs and returned in a few minutes with a helpless boy between them.

Wentworth stared at him and his eyes grew narrow and hard and his mouth straightened into a thin knife-blade of anger. He knew that tousled blond hair, that freckle-sprinkled face. It was young Jim Walsh. Memory of another face flashed across his mind, the dead face of a boy who had been tortured with white-hot metal. His head swung toward the woman.

"Why do you war on children?" he demanded harshly. "The kid can't possibly have done anything to warrant such treatment."

The woman's smile did not alter.

"That's what you think," she said sweetly. "Young Curley and this little rat brought you into the case and you killed four of my best men."

The boy was dropped roughly to the floor. He twisted his white, freckled face about, staring at the naked Wentworth, staring at the woman. She turned her head and glanced at him across her shoulder.

"This naked man over here is the Spider, kid," she said. "I wish you the joy of his company. Unfortunately I can allow you only fifteen minutes of it."

Wentworth squirmed on the floor until he could brace his shoulders against the wall and face the woman better. The muscles were knotted across his powerful chest. Cords bulged in his tanned shoulders, and he clipped out words between clenched teeth.

"Listen, woman," he began.

"Call me Captain Kidd," she said, still sweetly.

"Listen, woman," Wentworth said violently. "Do anything you want to me, but turn the kid loose. He can't hurt anyone. I'll buy his life. Give me my checkbook and I'll pay you whatever you say."

The woman smiled with her lips, her eyes nasty. "We don't need your money, Spider," she said. "After tonight, your dollars will be too picayune to bother with."

After tonight! Wentworth caught at the words. God in heaven, what atrocity could not the woman plan with her chained lightnings? He must get free, must warn the unsuspecting public.

"What do you mean?" he asked heavily.

The woman shook her head slowly, still smiling with her mouth. "That is one of your favorite tricks, isn't it, Spider?" she mocked. "To place your enemy in such a position that he is sure of your death and so not afraid to brag of what he will do? But this time, Spider, it won't work. For two reasons; the first is, I won't talk; the second is, *you won't escape!*"

She walked with lithely swaying hips across the room to where a number of wires bunched from an insulator on the wall. She took two of them and inspected their ends. The rubber insulation had been peeled back for a full two feet and the copper gleamed. She smiled as she minced toward Wentworth, bent and twisted the bared copper of one wire tight about his left biceps.

Wentworth did not look now at what she did—the touch of her fingers on his flesh, the bite of the wire told him that—but stared with horror at her close, dark face. He felt revulsion from her hands as against the cold touch of a snake in the dark, and panic beat against his ribs, panic in the man who knew no fear! The woman was fastening the other wire to his leg just below the knee now, and he knew what these wires signified. She meant to shoot the deadly Green Fire through his body!

"Too bad, Spider," she sighed.

HER TRAILING fingers left his flesh and she strode deliberately to the boy, fastened a wire to each of his arms. She snatched up a two-gallon can then and poured liquid from it over the boy. He ducked and fought his bonds, but he was too closely tied and Wentworth caught the strangling acrid smell of kerosene!

Despite himself, he shuddered. Was there no end to the fiendishness of this woman! She was not satisfied with sending the searing flame of the Green Fire through their bodies but she must burn them in oil as well! He twisted his head away from the jet of the oil as she spewed it over his own body. He coughed violently, choked by the rising fumes, watched through streaming eyes as the woman spilled a trail of kerosene across the floor and dropped the bared end of still another wire into a pool of it. She turned and smiled at Wentworth.

"Get the picture, Spider?" she jeered.

Wentworth said hoarsely, "For God's sake, not the boy!"

He knew there was no hope, but he was playing for time, fighting those bonds that gnawed as if with living files into his wrists, for time to contrive a way out of this fearsome death trap.

The woman frowned impatiently. "Don't be a fool, Spider," she said roughly. "You know both of you must die. I'm sure you get the picture all right, but I think I'll explain a little." She was gloating, rolling words over her tongue, glorying in the helplessness of this Master of Men. "There's a switch box on the road about fifteen minutes drive from here. When I reach that I'll pull the switch and you two will get a taste of the Green Fire. Also the house will be set on fire. If you get away from those two little devices of mine, you're much better than you're supposed to be, Spider. And much, much better than you seem to be."

She laughed. "Why don't I just shoot you?" she asked, reading his thoughts. "It's like this, Spider. Someone might know the task those four detectives set out to perform. If they come looking for the dicks, I want them to find the remains of two bodies here—your own—so that they'll think we died in our own trap. And bullets, dear Spider, have a way of embedding themselves in bones and even surviving fire."

She looked calmly over her victims and Wentworth, frantic, cried out:

"But, Captain Kidd, not the boy! Don't kill the boy that way!"

The woman threw back her head, laughed again, mockingly, and turned away into the night.

Wentworth's mind was grappling futilely with the problem of escape. Was this the finish of the Spider's crusades? Must they end in a blast of searing flame and the tearing agony of death? Somewhere, sometime, he knew, the Spider must fall in his ceaseless battling with crime and injustice, but to die with the enemy triumphant! To die when such fearful peril menaced the world!

He lifted his head and stared about him, met the dumb appeal in the eyes of the boy and could give him no hope. It looked like trail's end for the Spider.

CHAPTER 6
MODERN PIRACY

OUTSIDE, THE woman, Captain Kidd, walked briskly to a limousine that waited in the black night. A quarter mile away the headlights of other cars and a truck funneled whitely into the darkness.

The car slid forward, purring. The woman picked up her white cat from the cushions and dropped it into her lap, fingers combing in its long hair.

Richard Wentworth

"Stop at the switch," she said, saw the chauffeur's head nod blackly against the headlight glare and settled back into the cushions. Fifteen minutes later the car edged to the left of the road. The woman got out and fumbled at the base of an oak tree. She found a small box, opened it and revealed a small electric switch. She stared at it with wide, steady eyes, then sighed a little, lifted her shoulders in a small shrug and closed the switch with a firm, positive thrust.

While a man might have counted ten she held it so, then she yanked the box loose from its wires and carried it with her back to the car.

"Stop at the crest of the next hill," she said.

The car lounged on a hundred yards and halted and she peered toward the old farmhouse on the hill. Yellow flames were licking out of the doors and windows, lapping at the ancient wood. The woman smiled slowly, and small white teeth showed between the venomous red of her lips. She touched her fingers to her mouth and blew a kiss.

"Bye-bye, Spider," she said. "May you roast in hell."

Her voice was hard. For another long moment she stared at the mounting flames, then she settled comfortably into the cushions, picked up the cat again.

An hour later the car halted amid a group of men standing

closely together in the dark. One of them stepped up to the limousine.

"On time, Chief," he reported.

"That's fine," she said softly. "But remember, I want every man finished with his job and off the train in five minutes flat. Tell them, Bolo, that at the end of five minutes, the Green Fire will be turned on again."

"You mean that, Chief?" he asked.

Her voice cut like a knife. "I do," she snapped. "How long do you think a train like that can remain stationary on the main line without that fact being discovered? If a single man delays us, the trucks won't get away in time. Spread that word: when five minutes are up the Green Fire goes on! The sooner we eliminate the inefficient the better. Help me out of here. I want to see everything."

The door opened, and the man's bulky figure loomed in the dark. He stood a head taller than the woman and was broad in the shoulders. He caught her arm and helped her up the sharp slope.

"Glasses, Bolo, my darling," said the woman. There was an eager catch in her breath. The glasses revealed the glittering quadruple rails of a double-tracked railway right of way below.

"How long?" she queried.

"About two minutes," growled the man called Bolo.

"They arranged three contacts?" she asked next. "We want to make absolutely sure that everybody dies."

Bolo nodded heavily. "Terry said that instead of fastening the wires to the rails, he was fixing it up like he did that automobile trap. You know, two stiff wires sticking up so they touch the coaches themselves."

"That's better," the woman breathed. "The coaches are steel, and the insulation in the wheel trucks can't interfere."

"I don't know nothing about that," Bolo growled, "but they got three sets of wires like that stuck up along the rails. They'll keep the Green Fire on as long as they're touching. About fifty feet after the end of the train passes one set of wires, the loco-motive will run into the next set, Terry says."

As if that were a signal, a whistle wailed off in the distance, wailed twice more, mournfully, and died. The woman licked her lips, hands tight on the glasses.

The blue-white gleam of a headlight built a glow about the shoulder of the hill where she watched the bend. The glow brightened. The light's eye pushed around the bend and thrust a brilliant finger off into the night. The woman's hand closed on Bolo's muscle-knotted forearm. Her fingers bit in deeply.

"Now," she whispered. *"Now!…"*

WITHIN THE train, all was peace and quiet. The overhead lights were dim and the green curtains hung heavy and dark, swaying now and then to the rhythm of the speeding Inland Limited. The gray-haired conductor walked slowly through the dimness, stopped a moment in the doorway of the men's smoker and glanced in at the white-coated porter, busily shining shoes.

The conductor pushed on along into the car proper and looked weary-eyed along the swaying aisle. Somewhere a baby, awake in the night, gurgled. A mother murmured soft, lulling words—as on the hill the woman gripped Bolo's arm and hissed, "Now! Now!"

The conductor was smiling, his ears filled with the mother's soft humming when, like the fury of hell, the Green Fire struck! It struck like lightning, like a bolt from blue, cloudless skies. The dim, sleeping aisle of the Pullman glittered suddenly with livid light. Green-white chains of flame that struck like vicious snakes stabbed out from every metal thing upon the train, from the steel sides of the coaches.

The old conductor's face twitched convulsively and the chained lightning of the killers danced in fiendish glee. In the smoker, the Negro porter writhed upon the floor. In their berths, men and women and children tossed and jerked in the torturing grip of incredibly powerful voltage. And everywhere through the train the green, horrible light wavered and danced.

Then the light faded. The lamps of the train were burned out. Deep darkness settled over the Pullman and there was no sound at all save the clicking of the rails, the small whispering creaks of the speeding train. Then the green-white flare leaped again. The conductor and the mother and the child lay dead on the floor, electrocuted by that first fierce flash of Green Fire. Their dead bodies jerked to the stabbing of this new torture. They and all that cargo of corpses were ready now for the looters, ready for the woman who waited on the hill, watching avidly through her glasses, her small pink tongue touching dry excited lips.

SHE WATCHED while the third searing flash of the Green Fire made the night blaze with livid fire. From where she stood, she watched it dance like Northern Lights about the oncoming train. The locomotive was aflame with it, every car became a living wavering mass of the spitting snake tongues of the Green Fire. For ten seconds more this third flash of the fire danced, then final darkness fell.

Still the unlighted train roared on. There was no sound save the steady drumming of the exhaust, the click and humming of the rails. The woman's fingers gouged Bolo's arm until the nails drew blood.

The train was slowing. Air hissed and steam spurted from the engine in white clouds. Opposite the hill on which the woman stood, it halted and a man, visible in the back glow of a firebox, waved a cheery hand.

"Terry came through all right!" the woman said, sucking in her breath with audible relief. "His insulation trick worked as well as the three wire contacts." She laughed, horribly. "A medal for Terry!"

The man leaning from the locomotive cab shouted, and Captain Kidd, listening tensely, heard the words dimly, like echoes:

"Come—and—get—it!"

She took her hand from Bolo's arm.

"Go!" she said curtly, the passion drained from her voice. "In five minutes, remember, the train backs into that last contact, and the Green Fire dances again! I'll tell Terry to take up two contacts and leave one."

The hulk of a man went down the hill with long, heavy strides, crashing through underbrush, leaping a stream bed. He scrambled up the low slope of loose gravel to the right of way, swung in an opened Pullman door and threw his torch along its side. From all directions, men with flashlights were swarming on the train. A crew already labored in the mail and baggage cars, tossing bags and trunks, sacks of mail into the waiting trucks that had backed up along a rutty small road.

"Five minutes!" The man called Bolo shouted.

He put his hands to his mouth as a megaphone and stumped through the cars shouting, "Five minutes. In five minutes the Green Fire goes on again. Five minutes!"

He was built like a Greek wrestler, a mountainous man six feet four or five inches tall with a bristling black beard in which his mouth was a black gap as he shouted. All about him men worked with mad speed, robbing the dead.

Bolo drew out a huge silver watch and stared at it. Quarter past two. He looked about him with small, red-rimmed eyes. A diminutive, shriveled man yanked aside the green curtains of a Pullman berth.

"Ain't she a beauty?" he chuckled and leaned into the berth.

A girl of twenty-two or three lay there with the covers tucked neatly in about her, her white round arms lying on the coverlet. Her left hand was a fist and on it a large diamond sparkled. The small man grabbed her wrist and tugged at the fingers. They wouldn't open. He snarled, cursing vilely.

"Cut it off," said Bolo impassively. "You ain't got long."

A knife gleamed and slashed the dead hand. The little man wrenched the finger back until the bone snapped, hacked at it again and dropped finger and ring into a pouch that swung in front of him. Hurriedly he skimmed over bags, felt under the pillow. A half dozen men were busy in the car.

Bolo looked at his watch. Two minutes had elapsed. He yanked aside the green curtains of an upper berth. An old woman lay there, a book upon her chest. She had been reading when the Green Fire struck. Diamonds dangled below her gray hair. Bolo reached up and ripped the baubles out of the old woman's pierced ears. He found a pocketbook stuffed with money.

Three minutes gone now. He shouted that information, and the ghouls repeated his cry. Bolo strode into the next car. A strong worker had been busy here. Corpses were tumbled in pitifully contorted confusion on the floor. Men and young girls. A baby lying flat on its back, its legs doubled and crossed as if it still played in death. Its tight hand grasped with clumsy fingers a ring with a nipple attached to it.

The body of the aged conductor knelt grotesquely, face and knees upon the floor. A young girl sprawled naked in the aisle, her flimsy silken pajamas torn from her by marauding hands. Bedding was tumbled in the floors by the frantic swift search for valuables. Bolo curiously lifted a blanket and revealed a young mother with a child close in her arms. The bearded man looked at his watch.

"Four minutes!" he shouted. "All out!"

HIS CRY echoed down the car, was picked up by another man in the next car. The shriveled little man ducked out of the last berth, holding the arm of a woman. The hand was rich with rings. He lifted a heavy knife above his head and whacked down on the wrist. The knife dug in and stuck in the bone. He wrenched it violently, cursing, jerked the knife free and sliced down again. The hand came off and he scuttled toward the door with it in his fist. Bolo glanced at his watch and reached an exit in two great strides, swung to the earth.

"Fifteen seconds to go!" he shouted.

He scrambled down the gravel embankment. Everywhere men were tumbling from the train. The locomotive exhaust barked and the coaches creaked slowly backward. Many men were already crashing through the underbrush toward the roaring motors of the get-away cars. Bolo toiled slowly up the hill toward the woman. Somewhere a man cried hoarsely.

"Wait!" he shouted. "Wait!"

Green Fire turned the night livid again. It danced and quivered in the air, radiating from the train in leaping sparks of green and white and violet blue. For moments it continued, then, as sudden as death, it was gone. Bolo, eyes blinded by the brilliance, stumbled on to where the woman waited.

"Looks like one of our boys got caught," he said gruffly.

The woman laughed hissingly in the dark. "Next time, they'll work faster. Take me to my car."

Without a word, the huge man led her down a narrow, steep path and handed her into the car.

"Get in," she said crisply, and he squeezed his bulk into the tonneau, sat gingerly on the deep cushions. He sat staring straight ahead of him. He was silent while the car backed and swung into the road, purred off with mounting speed.

Finally the woman spoke beside him.

"Not getting squeamish, Bolo?"

The man turned a slow head toward the woman he could not see in the darkness.

"No," he said heavily. "It's just that I didn't see Bill. I'm hoping the greedy fool isn't the one got caught on the train."

The woman smiled with her red lips like snakes, switched on a small light which threw a subdued light upward into their faces. Her left hand was in a small bag she held in her lap and the hand was pointed in Bolo's direction.

"No," she said softly. "Bill didn't come here tonight."

Bolo still stared at her with his small, red-rimmed eyes. The black beard hid most of his face and his eyes expressed nothing.

"Bill," said the woman, "is dead. He used an emergency device unnecessarily and made it necessary to destroy our hiding place near Scarsdale."

The man continued to look at her unblinkingly. "You mean he got killed?" His voice was dull.

"Yes," said the woman. "He got killed. I shot him." The wrist of the white hand that was hidden in the bag stiffened a little, the bag lifted from her lap so that it pointed toward the big man's chest.

The big man blinked slowly. "You know Bill was my brother," he said heavily.

"I know Bill was your brother."

The big man nodded, still staring directly into her eyes.

"But Bill always was an ornery skunk," he said. "I was afraid he would get us into trouble. Good thing you caught him so soon."

The woman held his gaze with her dark eyes. "You are wise, Bolo," she said softly, "very wise."

The big man grunted and swung his bearded, impassive face forward.

"Millions," she continued. "Millions and millions. And not a chance of being caught, Bolo, *as long as we kill all the witnesses!* That was how the pirates worked in the old days. They killed all the witnesses and all of them got rich and some lived to enjoy the riches… You and I will live, Bolo, *whatever happens to the rest!*"

The big man's head swung around swiftly. He stared into her eyes again. "Whatever happens to the rest?" He said it softly, too, as if he feared that the man ahead of them would hear. "Do you mean—" He broke off with a half-frightened curse. "You little witch!"

The woman leaned back in her corner of the cushions. The big man pushed his bearded face close.

"You mean you and I," he said, "would throw the switch—in less than five minutes!"

The woman laughed and laughed.

CHAPTER 7
FIRE TRAP

THE INSTANT the woman who called herself Captain Kidd had left the room where Wentworth and the boy lay bound and helpless in her death trap, Wentworth went to work on his bonds. Ropes bit tightly into his wrists and were tied up short to an iron ring in the wall. He could not squirm around to get at that with his teeth. His feet were bound also and about an arm and leg had been twisted copper wire with the insulation scraped clean, copper wire that within fifteen minutes would sear his flesh with Green Fife and electrocute him!

A single, dangling electric light bulb, bare on a cord, illuminated the room, and by its yellow, direct glare, Wentworth studied their prison. He quickly found that his own position was hopeless, and at once began to study that of the boy. Jimmy Walsh was tied in exactly the same way. The boy stared at him with wide, trustful eyes. He grinned.

"Let's go, Spider," he said. "When do we get out of here?"

Wentworth grinned back at him. "That may be up to you, son," he said. "They tied me up pretty tight here. Pull on your ring and see how tightly they fastened you to it."

The boy twisted his head and stared at the iron ring that, just above his head, held the end of the rope that bound him. It was too close for him to do more than peer at it out of the corner of his eye, too close for him to get at it with his teeth.

"It don't look so strong," he said.

"Put your weight against it," Wentworth ordered swiftly, "and work fast."

The boy heaved his weight forward, tugging on the rope. Wentworth watched with anxious eyes. He saw the ring twisting and wrenching in its socket, thought he saw it slip a fraction of an inch.

The boy was panting with the strain now. If he could get a

little additional leverage on that ring… Swiftly Wentworth glanced upward at the wires that were to bring their death. He knew how tough those wires were. There would be no chance to snap them by pulling. He studied their fastening. They were wrapped around an ordinary white insulator, a single rusty nail through its core.

A thrill of hope shot through Wentworth. The wires that led to the boy and himself were twisted together around that single insulator. If he could pull that fastening loose, the boy could drag the wires to him and, with that link between them, he and Wentworth could throw their combined weight against the ring that held the boy prisoner.

Once the boy was free to roll to Wentworth, it would be a simple matter to gnaw through Jim's bonds and permit him to escape. At least, he would be able to save this boy who faced horrible death because he had sought to help the Spider. With luck and fast work, Wentworth, too, might get out of his death trap. But he must be quick!

"Keep on trying," Wentworth told the boy and, leaning forward, then back, looping the wires that menaced him about his shoulders, he managed to pull them tight in their stretch from the insulator to himself. He twisted again, trying to wrap the wires about his shoulders and succeeded only in getting his head through the loop. They pressed tautly against his throat, but they were straining at the insulator too. He threw his whole weight against the wires. The thin cables cut against his throat, shut off his wind. He increased the pressure.

"What you doing, Spider?" the boy cried, eyes frightened. "Don't kill yourself, Spider! We'll get loose!"

FOR AN instant the wires tightened excruciatingly about Wentworth's neck, then they went limp and he sagged in his bonds, wind whistling in his throat, hissing through his clenched teeth. The congested blood drained slowly from his face and after a minute he lifted his head heavily.

Blackness still clouded his vision, the humming of the blood was still in his ears, but he had no time to spare in resting. His battle was only a third won. God alone knew whether he could win the other two thirds before that hell-cat of a woman threw the switch there on the road, shot killing electricity through their bodies. For Wentworth had not broken the wires. He had only pulled them loose from the insulator!

He fought to get words through his aching throat. His tongue moved stiffly.

"Jim," he gasped out finally. "Get wire in teeth. Pull to you.

"Hurry!" Wentworth said hoarsely.

The boy snapped himself out of his paralysis of surprise and seized in his teeth the wires that were fastened to one of his arms, dragged them toward him. Wentworth twisted his neck clear of the wire, shook his head violently to help circulation. When he spoke again, the words came freely, though still hoarsely.

"This is the plan, Jim," he said. "No, don't stop! Keep on pulling on the wire. When you get the insulator to you, I want you to wrap the wire that is fastened to me around your body—" he forced a grim smile—"not around your neck as I did. When you have done that, you and I will pull together on that ring. I think that together we'll be able to pull it loose. Then you'll be able to get over where I can gnaw your ropes in two. But hurry!"

The boy grunted, but did not stop his pulling at the wire. He leaned forward as far as possible and bit the wire, then leaned back and tilted his head upward to drag the wire toward him. Then he lunged forward again.

Three minutes of that, and he reached the wire that was fastened to Wentworth's arm. Immediately he began to tangle himself in it so that it would be taut between the Spider and himself.

Wentworth grinned. "Ready? This may hurt you, Jim."

He threw his weight backward on the wires that held them together, and Jim pulled with his full strength. The wires bit into Wentworth's arm. He could see them tighten and strain into the boy's flesh, saw the boy's face go pale with the pain. But there could be no delay, no gentleness here. It was this or death.

The staple that held the ring to which Jim was tied grated in the wood, but did not yield. Wentworth relaxed the strain.

"Heave," he grunted. "Right! Now left! Heave again."

Together to his panted orders, the two of them fought the staple, until Wentworth felt his own arms go numb with the tourniquet of the wire, until Jim was pale to fainting from pain.

Wentworth eased off. "Rest a second," he gasped out. "Now, one last strong heave."

Together they wrenched and Wentworth slammed against

the wall and heard the protesting shriek as the iron yielded. Two thirds of the way to freedom!

"Roll to me," he cried. "Roll, fast. We can't have many minutes left!"

HE HEARD Jim floundering on the floor, and lurched erect, leaning forward to get to the boy at the first possible instant. Jim was half crawling, half rolling, toward Wentworth, fighting free of the entangling wires as he came. He made a final half roll and thrust his hands, tied behind him, within reach of Wentworth's mouth.

For a fleeting instant Wentworth studied the ropes, then he began to tug at one end with his teeth. It was heart-breaking, gum-tearing work, but finally the rope yielded and within moments Jim fought a hand free of the rope.

"Don't wait to untie the ropes," Wentworth gasped out, "get both those wires off you. A touch of one of them will kill. Your body and this cork will form a ground."

The boy twisted around on his bound arms and went to work on the wire on Wentworth's arm, tugging at it with his one, half-numbed hand.

"Yourself first!" Wentworth snapped angrily.

"If you don't hold still," the boy said stubbornly, "you're going to burn us both."

Wentworth held still then, eyes gentle with admiration for the bravery of this small boy who so willingly risked his own life that he should survive. But it was not Wentworth, it was the Spider who must survive, survive to wreak vengeance, to stop the fiendish depredations of this vile woman and her chained lightning!

At last one wire came loose from Wentworth's arm and the boy flung himself at the other. Wentworth exclaimed, "I'm a fool. Don't bother to untwist it, work it back and forth until it breaks."

The boy nodded and began to do that without words. Wentworth stared out the open door while the thin torn fingers fumbled with the wire. In the distance he saw headlights boring through the night, saw those headlights stop!

A hoarse cry escaped him. "She's stopped. In a minute, the current...."

The boy gasped, "There," and snapped the wire clean on Wentworth's leg.

"Work on that wire on your left arm," Wentworth ordered, "I'll take the right."

While the boy fumbled with the wire, Wentworth seized the electrode on the boy's right arm in his teeth and twisted it frantically, back and forth.

"Please don't, Spider," the boy pleaded, his voice near tears. "You'll kill yourself, biting that wire when she turns on the current. Don't! Don't!"

Wentworth continued to jerk his head back and forth, tugging at the wire, twisting it, wrenching it to break the metal in two while the boy's hand worked on his left arm. With a final wrench, Wentworth tugged at the wire and lunged backward, spitting the end of the wire from his mouth. The boy threw the other wire clear at the same instant, rolled backward—and flame spat from the dangling ends of the cables!

GREEN-WHITE FLAME licked the floor, touched it to instant leaping fire. Yellow smoky tongues spurted up from each spot where the wires touched.

The boy had flung himself against Wentworth now, working on the knots that still bound him. Flames lapped higher. A draft through the open door fanned the hungry fire toward them. Neither Wentworth nor the boy spoke now, both struggling frantically with the bonds. The flames were creeping closer. Wentworth's body was drenched with the oil and the boy's clothing was dripping with it. The flames licked closer. A spark lit on the boy's back, and a minute spire of flame leaped up.

Wentworth pressed it out with his bare chest, and an instant later the rope slipped from his right hand. He jerked loose from the ring that bound him to the wall. His left hand and his legs were still bound, as were the boy's, but they could not delay.

"Don't wait for any more," Wentworth panted out. "The back window there, roll to it and fall out. It isn't high."

He and the boy dragged themselves toward the window. The house was oven-hot about them. Sparks were roaring upward. Black smoke, laden with oil fumes, nearly strangled them. Wentworth twice beat out sparks that lit on the inflammable clothing of the boy. His own body, less absorbent, had had time to shed the oil before the fire burst out.

The boy reached the window and hung there panting. He struggled to lift himself to the sill, but his already overtaxed strength failed. He clung there grimly. Wentworth reached his side with a frantic lurch and roll. With his one free hand, he boosted the boy upward, shoved him out, and swarmed over the sill himself by the leverage of his one arm. Looking down, he waited until Jim rolled clear before he dropped to the ground.

Wentworth and the boy, clear of the scorching area of heat, rapidly untied each other's bonds and together, a naked, grim-faced man and a weary boy with worship in his eyes, hurried afoot across the fields to rouse the world against a new horror.

It took an hour to reach a house after they found Wentworth's taxi had been taken. It was half an hour later before Jim had been able to get clothing for Wentworth, and he, in turn, was able to persuade the man of the house to drive him to police headquarters. It was two and a half hours after they escaped the fire trap that the car squeaked to a halt in Center Street and Wentworth dashed into headquarters with Jim trailing him.

He met Kirkpatrick storming out, saturnine face set and angry. Wentworth seized him by the arm.

"Kirk," he cried, "we must hurry! A new gang, armed with chained lightning, is going to strike tonight!"

Kirkpatrick halted in his stride to stare at Wentworth with a strained face.

"They've already struck," he said sharply. "I just got a flash that a cargo of corpses had crashed at full speed into Grand Central station!"

CHAPTER 8
WHOLESALE SLAUGHTER

WENTWORTH SWUNG about and paced beside Kirkpatrick. Jim Walsh trotted along beside them, staring up so fixedly into Wentworth's face that he almost fell when they reached the broad steps leading down to Center Street.

Wentworth thrust the boy first into the big police phaeton and piled in ahead of Kirkpatrick. The car lurched forward, rounded the corner into Lafayette at forty-five and before it reached the next corner was doing seventy with the siren howling madly, wide open.

Above its fury, Wentworth shouted at Kirkpatrick the information he had gleaned from Jim Walsh; that the boy had learned through Jack Curley, grandson of the inventor, that gangsters had forced the old man to yield model and detailed plans of a small but extremely powerful transformer; that he had been coerced and kept silent by the kidnaping of his granddaughter, Nellie.

Jim had been seized just as he had left Kirkpatrick's home and taken to the place where Wentworth afterward had seen the terrible beauty of the woman pirate who called herself Captain Kidd.

As he finished, the police car streaked down past the viaduct of Park Avenue and whirled into Forty-second Street before the imposing mass of the Grand Central station. The car snubbed to a halt and Kirkpatrick flung out and strode long-legged past crowds of gawking people held back by the tight blue lines of police. He slapped through swing doors, and stalked into the deserted station with Wentworth and the boy at his heels.

The high, vaulted ceiling echoed weirdly to their solitary footsteps. The usually crowded concourse was empty except for the scurrying passage of two men in white who carried a stretch-

The entire train had crashed at full speed into the station.

er between them. The sheet that covered the stretcher had a spreading stain of red.

Wentworth pivoted. "Jim, you better stay here."

The boy's freckles stood out vividly on his pale face.

"I can take it, Sp—!" Wentworth's quick frown stopped him, and he finished, "Specially if I'm along with you."

Wentworth's lids half concealed his eyes and a small smile of pleasure at the boy's alertness crossed his lips. He clapped a hand on Jim's back affectionately.

"Okay, Jim, come along."

They pounded after the bobbing, fast-moving figure of Kirkpatrick and overtook him on the downward stairs into a low tunnel. Sound began to drift up to him, screams and sobs echoing in the confined space. A double guard of police saluted and stepped aside.

The three swung to the right around a buttress and Wentworth slammed into Kirkpatrick standing rigid as a rock. Wentworth stepped aside and a gasp of horror grated between his teeth. A locomotive lay upon its battered side on the platform, the cars crumpled behind it as if squeezed in some Titan's vise. Some sprawled upon their sides. One, upended, had ridden over the car ahead and its huge steel trucks threatened momentary death to those who labored below. A porter's red cap lay upon the platform upside down. A leg clad in black with a red stripe down its side thrust out from beneath an overturned car. A dark, viscous pool spread beside that leg.

WENTWORTH THRUST Jim behind him. An inspector of police with lips grim in a gray face strode up to Kirkpatrick.

"It's not an accident, Kirk," he reported sharply. "I went inside to help the injured and there was nothing we could do. They were dead, everyone of them. The doctor says they were electrocuted."

"The whole trainload?" Horror and incredulity made Kirkpatrick's voice strained.

"The whole trainload," the inspector said grimly. "The safety devices on the locomotive were smashed and the train ran full-tilt into the station with a dead man at the throttle!"

Wentworth put Jim Walsh in a policeman's care and he and Kirkpatrick went slowly through the cars that still stood upright, saw the horror that Bolo had surveyed unflinching a brief while before. They came out feeling sick and weak. On the platform the two men stared into each other's eyes. Wentworth was the first to find his voice.

"You see now why she called herself Captain Kidd?" he demanded grimly. *"They kill all the witnesses.* There is no one left alive to tell how this horror is contrived. If it had not been for Jim Walsh telling us of that stolen transformer, we would be without any explanation of how these passengers were electrocuted in their berths."

Kirkpatrick was frowning. "But the trains are insulated against currents."

"Against normal currents," Wentworth conceded, "but not against any such power as I saw loosed by those wires stretched across a country road. Autos are insulated from the road by rubber tires and yet that carload of detectives was burned down in an instant and the auto itself bristled with green and white sparks of electric fire." He pointed to a scorched scratch that extended the length of the steel coach beside which they stood.

"Evidently, they used the same system in attacking the train that they employed against the auto."

Together the two white-faced men strode from the platform and Jim Walsh broke from the policeman's hands and ran with them. Up the long echoing ramps they went again and out into the open, moved to the waiting police phaeton at the curb. Jim was the first to scramble inside.

"Wuxtra!" a newsboy bawled from the crowd. "Wuxtra! All about the big train wreck; Noo Joisey train wrecked in tunnel!"

Wentworth got hold of a paper, went swiftly back to Kirkpatrick's side. By the light of a pocket flashlight, they read the shrieking black headlines, four lines of three-inch type across the page.

TRAIN WRECKS KILL 1,000;
PENNSY FLIER CRASHES IN TUBE;
2ND SMASH IN GRAND CENTRAL;
FIVE MAIL PLANES CRACK UP.

Wentworth's hand knotted into a rock-hard fist. He could barely force words from his throat.

"And the loot will run into millions," he said slowly. "Millions—and a thousand witnesses killed. Captain Kidd—does—right—well."

He looked blankly at the face of an illuminated clock on the corner. Its hands stood at seven minutes of three.

CHAPTER 9
STRANDS OF THE WEB

WENTWORTH TURNED his head heavily toward Kirkpatrick, then Jim Walsh's shrill voice broke into the silence.

"The paper says they found two of them mail pilots and they had been electrocuted," Jim said again. "It's Captain Kidd working out there, too."

Wentworth nodded heavily. The car droned south along the Park Avenue viaduct, on into Fourth Avenue.

"Kirk," he said slowly, "there are three things that might give us a clue to the operators of this damnable chained lightning. One is this granddaughter of Curley who was kidnapped. Her name is Nellie Curley. Jim here can give you a description. He says that she has been going around lately with Dutch Brogard. He's a gunman half the force should know by sight. Another lead is the patent corporations which Curley may have consulted about his transformer. A dick of the Black Agency trailed me tonight and I had a run-in with him. That might help, too."

Kirkpatrick nodded. "I'll get men on those things. What are you going to do?"

Wentworth smiled wearily. "I'm going to see Nita."

The police commissioner stared at him with curiously kind eyes. "Dick, aren't you—" he hesitated.

Wentworth frowned. "What is it, Kirk?"

Kirkpatrick said clearly, "Why the devil don't you and Nita get married? If ever I saw two fools crazy about each other!"

Wentworth did not look at Kirkpatrick, nor did he think it strange that the words should come from his friend. It was sheer reaction against so much horror that the mind should veer from the track of fearfulness, turn into some other much-worn path.

"Nita prefers her freedom," Wentworth said carefully.

"Baloney!" exploded Kirkpatrick.

Wentworth turned abruptly, a clenched fist on his knee, his face displaying such emotion as he never permitted in his guarded moments. This thing had caught him on the raw. His mouth was tight.

Kirkpatrick clapped an affectionate hand on Wentworth's shoulder. "I'm sorry; I spoke without thinking." He leaned forward and caught the speaking tube that communicated with the uniformed chauffeur.

"Drop me at headquarters," he ordered, "Then take Mr. Wentworth to Riverside Tower."

He turned to Jim Walsh, and a few minutes later, when he left them, the Police Commissioner of New York City had a detailed description of the kidnapped Nell Curley.

In twenty minutes the car dropped Wentworth and the boy at the apartment house, Riverside Tower, which reared a high square peak into the night sky, black against the east where showed the first gray hint of dawn.

A SLEEPY elevator operator shot them far upward and Wentworth crossed the hall, touched a white bell button. A buzzer sounded remotely and within moments the door was flung wide and Nita van Sloan held out her hands to Wentworth.

"I've been expecting you, Dick," she said calmly, her blue eyes warm with welcome. She glanced toward the boy, put a hand on his tousled blond head. A big head thrust out from behind her and a Great Dane dog that romped like a puppy, wagging its tail violently, pranced about Wentworth, licking his hand.

"Down, Apollo," Wentworth ordered. He threw an arm about Nita's shoulders and walked into the apartment. The dog pranced ahead of them, head with lolling tongue twisting about to see the master he loved. Nita's other arm was about Jim Walsh and when they were within the lamp-lighted sprawling apartment with its huge studio window open to the starry north sky, she stooped before the boy, smiling into his eyes.

"Dick has told me about you," she said. "You're the young man who saved him when those wicked people were setting buildings on fire everywhere. I never have thanked you for that because we couldn't let anybody know his real name."

The boy's face crinkled in an embarrassed grin, his eyes not meeting hers, his feet shuffling on the deep-piled rug.

"Aw, heck," he said, "I didn't do nothing."

Wentworth, sitting heavy-headed on a window seat, hands clasped between his knees, looked at the two of them and felt a suffocating pain rise up in his heart. Nita kneeling before a young boy, Nita lovely as always in the sweeping graceful folds of her black negligee with the boy's hands between her palms, her curly short hair of chestnut and gold close to that tousled boy's head, that boy's dirty boy face…. He jerked his head aside and stared out into the night.

Kirkpatrick had wrought more havoc than he knew with

that simple question, the question many of their friends must ask themselves time and again. Why didn't Dick Wentworth and Nita van Sloan marry? Two such eminently suitable young people, so obviously crazy about each other. Why didn't they marry?

A curse squeezed out between Wentworth's teeth. As if the Spider could marry! As if any man with the weight of his crimes of justice upon his shoulders might wed! A man who never knew when the heavy hand of the law would fall upon his shoulder. Even tonight he had killed four men, men who richly deserved to die to be sure. But their death was murder in the eyes of the law, and the law cannot consider motives!

Wentworth jerked to his feet, strode across the room to where a violin case rested upon a grand piano. He caught up the instrument, brushed the strings to resonance with the bow and began to play.

Wilder and wilder the music soared into the night, such music as is given to few men to create. For Wentworth, if he had not chosen the harder way, might well have been lie leading virtuoso of the violin in all the world. It wracked the two who listened, the boy and the woman, side by side now. It was fearful stuff and torturing to the soul; lovely, yet frightful.

But presently the wildness went out of the soaring notes and the bowing grew slower and more slow and now it was beauty that droned from the strings. Haunting beauty was in the music, and Nita knew now that it was his love for her that he bespoke, love that was too deep for words, love that must ever deny itself. **WHEN, AN** hour later, Wentworth put down the violin, day was bright in the streets outside and the boy slumbered in Nita's arms. As Wentworth turned, she let the tired body slump down on the cushions of the davenport and crossed to the man's side.

"I called your home last night," she said quietly, "and they said you were out alone and that you wore the kit beneath your arm. They said you expected to be back early, that it was nothing serious."

A mocking smile twisted Wentworth's lips. "I was a fool," he said quietly. "More hell cut loose last night than I had dreamed was left in the world." He told her briefly what had happened, eyes intent on her hands clasped in his.

"I think our most important clue," he said finally, "is the fact that the girl who was kidnapped had been seen with Dutch Brogard. You know who he is, one of our most dapper gunmen. The police will be looking for both of them, but they will be working only on a verbal description of the girl. That's always tricky. I want you and Jim, who knows Nell well, to look over some night clubs. If you spot her or Dutch or any of his crowd, phone my home. I'll keep in touch that way."

Nita nodded slowly, smiled up into his face but her eyes were still worried. He kissed her and strode to the door. The Great Dane stalked with him and he dropped a hand on the massive head affectionately.

"Tell Jim I'll see him later," he called and was gone.

A half hour later he had picked the lock of the Black Detective Agency office and slipped inside. Broad daylight, yes, but for two hours or more these buildings would hold no life. The night's cleaning force had gone home and he would be undisturbed. Fifteen minutes, and the use of a small suction disc with ear tubes like a doctor's stethoscope, sufficed to open the safe and he pulled out the private files, seeking to learn who had set the detectives to trailing Jim Walsh.

The file of Ralph Donaghue, their operative, showed that the Patenteed Corporation of 120 Broad Avenue had been interested in Walsh!

Two hours later, Wentworth, disguised as he had been on the preceding night, entered the Patenteed offices and, pretending to be an employee of the Black Detective Agency, got to the manager, one Caspar Johnson. To him, Wentworth pointed out that the Pirates apparently were using the invention of the man the agency had been hired to investigate. He intimated that the agency was suspicious of Patenteed's motives.

Caspar Johnson demonstrated his thorough rascality, but convinced Wentworth he was not a party to the piratical atrocities that were threatening the country's people. Then the Spider gleaned one startling piece of information.

When Patenteed had attempted to obtain patents for the transformer, the company had learned that the invention already had been registered, and in the name of the kidnapped granddaughter, Nellie Curley!

The granddaughter was a known associate of a certain gangster. The patents on the transformer had been taken in her name and then she had been "kidnapped."

Old Jonas Curley could help him there. Wentworth laughed shortly as he strode from the building, sped toward the uptown hotel where he had told Curley to register.

In five minutes he was out again, racing toward Curley's tenement home, his face set and hard. Curley had never registered at the hotel.

That meant one of two things, Wentworth thought swiftly, as the taxi wove through traffic toward narrow, tawdry Bentley street. Either Curley had not trusted him and had remained at home; or he had been prevented by force from obeying. The taxi swerved to the curb and Wentworth took the tenement stairs two at a time. On the fourth floor, he knocked sharply on the door.

THERE WAS a long wait, then he heard feet shuffle toward the door. It opened and in the dim light, he made out the blonde head of the woman who last night had stood behind old Curley. His daughter, the gangster, Bill, had said. She wore loose house slippers and as she faced him, she snuffled from recent tears.

"I'm looking for Jonas Curley," Wentworth said rapidly. "I'm the man who gave him money last night and told him to go to a hotel…."

"Oh," the woman sobbed. "Oh, if only father had done what you said! I begged him to, but a little while after you left, a man came in with a gun and took him away!"

"And you didn't tell police?"

"I was afraid, afraid!" she cried.

Wentworth stood staring at the woman, his thoughts racing. He was remembering what that other woman who called herself Captain Kidd had said in her underground lair. Something about an old man she did not want to see. Take him away first, she had said. He cursed harshly. Of course! What a fool he had been! The gangsters had taken the old man as additional security. Jonas Curley had been a prisoner there in that farmhouse of horror, a prisoner of Captain Kidd!

Wentworth stared at the woman. She kept mopping her eyes with a wadded handkerchief. "You're Curley's daughter?" he asked slowly.

The woman nodded, sobbing aloud. "Oh, *oh!* I don't know what I'll do! I don't know. First little Nellie is kidnaped, then Jack is killed and now, now father...."

"Is Nellie your child?" Wentworth asked.

The blonde head shook. "My niece, she's an orphan, but I loved her so! Oh, if you can find her and father...."

Wentworth stood looking at the woman a moment longer, then he patted her awkwardly on a quivering shoulder. "There," he said, "it's hard, I know, but we'll find Mr. Curley for you, and your niece, too." He thrust money into her hand, turned and strode down the steps.

He had another line of attack against these land pirates and he must act on that at once. He stopped in the dim hall for a few moments to strip off his disguise, then sped to police headquarters.

There he was ushered immediately into the presence of Kirkpatrick who rose behind his desk, his face drawn with sleeplessness.

"Glad you came, Dick," he said as Wentworth strode energetically into the room. There was no weariness in Wentworth's face, only fresh eagerness. Swiftly he outlined what new facts he had learned about the granddaughter, Nellie Curley. "It's more important than ever that we locate Nellie," he said urgently. "It begins to look as if the girl might be behind all this crime, as if she had sold out her grandfather to the gang of her boyfriend, Dutch Brogard. Suppose we put a watch on the Curley home, too, just in case the gangsters should come after the daughter. She's the only one left now."

Kirkpatrick nodded quick agreement and Wentworth turned to his new angle of attack on the gangs. He drew out an air-line chart and indicated cross-marks that showed where planes had crashed with their pilots dead by electrocution.

"You notice," he said, "that every one of these crashes took place *off* the lane these planes normally would follow. And yet there were no storms to blow them off course."

Kirkpatrick frowned over the chart, supporting his tired head with his hand.

"Yes," he said, "that's true. Does that have any special meaning?"

Wentworth jerked his head in an affirmative. "I think so, Kirk. This is what I want you to do. While you prosecute the search for the girl here in the city, I want to take a mail plane west and see if I can't strike a blow directly at the Pirates themselves."

He explained rapidly then that he wanted to pose as an operative of the police department to be lent to the government for the trip. He would go in disguise as Detective Sergeant Cohalan, an identity he would create for this purpose alone.

Kirkpatrick nodded his head. Brightness was returning to his eyes now, the fatigue fading.

"Washington has had occasion to ask help of me a number of times," he said. "I don't doubt they'll reciprocate. But if you have to make arrests, Dick, you'll have to contact the local officials."

Wentworth smiled slowly, "Yes—if I have to make arrests," he said quietly.

CHAPTER 10
THE DEATH BEACON

WENTWORTH GLANCED out of the window of the special plane carrying mail westward from Wichita, Kansas, and saw a circling beacon of light glide by on their right. He checked the large map spread out on a board before him, glanced at an earth induction compass installed beside the board.

"Check," he said monotonously.

Wentworth's Hindu body-servant, Ram Singh, rose from where he squatted facing his master, his dark face utterly expressionless except for the bright idolatry of his eyes whenever they rested upon Wentworth. The Hindu stalked forward and poked his head into the forward cockpit.

"Check," he said.

Wentworth's eyes swung from chart and compass. They were fresh and there was no fatigue about him anywhere. He had slept three hours.

Kirkpatrick had been unable to get him a mail plane that he might pilot himself, but had arranged for a large cabin plane to carry the mail instead of the usual fast open cockpit ship, and Wentworth had a limited authority. His disguised face had the pale, flaccid look of a man who spends little time outdoors, who is awake much at night. There was more flesh on the cheeks than was natural and there were many wrinkles in his eye corners. Also his hair was graying. He was Detective Sergeant Cohalan. Before he had left New York on an early plane which had sped him to Wichita, he had arranged that the ordinary channels should know this plane was carrying valuable cargo—which it wasn't. That was to make sure the Pirates would strike.

At Wichita, the papers had screamed with lurid headlines, with demands that the government stop these forays of the modern pirates. Wentworth's eyes had gone haggard as he had read the fearful carnage that had been wrought. A Chesapeake and Ohio train, bound from Cincinnati to Richmond, had been the latest victim. Heaven only knew where the Pirates had struck, but the masterless train, plunging with mounting speed through the steep mountains of West Virginia, had leaped the track and sprawled its thirteen coaches over a jumbled, stony ravine.

The cars had spewed out corpses like split pods of peas, then fire had swept the wreck and it was the rosy glow of the funeral pyre of six hundred and forty-two dead—there had been day coaches in the train, too—that had brought discovery.

Government agents were working on the case, of course. Some were riding every train that carried valuable cargo—and some had died in that train that had tumbled its horror over the mountainside!

He kept the knife at his prisoner's back as
they climbed the wide cleats of the ladder.

No ordinary methods would avail against this pirate crew, Wentworth was sure. It would take the swift sword flash of the Spider to overcome them, a lightning-like attack that would match their own chained lightning. He studied the chart, glanced at his compass, and dashed forward.

"You're off the course," he barked at the pilot. "You're two degrees south of the course."

THE PILOT twisted a frowning face about, hands automatically swinging right and left on the wheel, working the aileron as the plane tilted in the air pumps.

"The radio beam is still clear," he said.

"Look at your compass," Wentworth snapped.

The man looked, shook his head. "Compass must be wrong. Radio is all right."

Wentworth frowned. It was true compasses wavered during flight, but those other planes....

"Steer by the compass," he ordered slowly.

"Listen. I'm piloting this plane," the pilot declared angrily.

Wentworth bent toward him, face set. "Those other planes that crashed were off their courses," he began swiftly.

The pilot snaked out a pistol. "Get out of the cockpit," he said sharply. "I believe you're one of these pirates and...."

Wentworth kicked the gun out of the man's hand, yanked him from his seat, and thrust him into Ram Singh's arms.

"Hold him," he ordered, as he sprang to the controls, and swung back on the compass course. The buzzing dots of the radio beam signals indicated he was swinging north off the route. He ignored that and slowly the beam faded.

The beat of the two powerful engines drowned all other sound and Wentworth gave his full attention to piloting, a difficult task by compass. Usually, pilots paid little heed to the compass when they were flying a laned course. The radio beacon guided them by means of a narrow beam which threw dots out at a close angle on one side of the course, dashes on the other. The pilot knew by the change in those signals—dots or dashes—when he varied from the true course.

Wentworth's face was grimly triumphant when presently on the true course, he caught the radio signals again. He raised his voice above the hammer of the engines.

"Bring the gentleman forward, Ram Singh." When the pilot,

his young face rigid with anger, was at his side again, Wentworth said swiftly:

"You see the compass indicates we are back on the course again. If you'll listen, you'll find the radio signals are all right." He smiled up at the pilot. "I'm sorry I had to do what I did, but I think you'll agree that I acted properly. As I held on this compass course, the radio signals coming in at the time indicated I was leaving the lane. They faded out after a while, then these signals came in. They conform with the compass course. Do you see what that means?"

Slowly the pilot's anger dwindled and a puzzled frown took its place.

"No, I don't," he said shortly.

Wentworth nodded gravely. "The only thing I can see is this. Somehow, those pirates set up a false radio beam—" he stopped abruptly, with a startled exclamation. "That's it!" he said. "Those same pirates that are looting the trains are leading planes off their course with a false beam! They use the same powerful transformer that they employ to electrocute the people on trains!"

The pilot's face was still hostile.

"I'll concede I acted a bit arbitrarily," Wentworth said, "but I didn't know how soon we might run into whatever is used to electrocute the pilots of planes and I had to act fast. Won't you take the plane now?"

Puzzlement and interest slowly dimmed the pilot's glare.

"You mean that was a *false* radio beam I was following?" he demanded. "But how is that possible?"

Ram Singh released him and he dropped into the co-pilot's seat, fitted the phones over his ears.

"I can't tell any difference," he began, then he cried, "These signals are weaker!"

Wentworth nodded, arising slowly. "Will you land, please, at the first field that has any phone or buildings on it?"

The pilot nodded, grinned. "Sorry I was so stubborn. Didn't know you were a pilot." Wentworth waved a hand in dismissal. He went back to his board and charted the exact spot and angle at which the plane had swung from the proper course.

AN HOUR later, but five thousand feet above the mail-plane level, Wentworth followed the false beams again in a small two-seater. Ram Singh was in the cockpit ahead, and with night glasses was sweeping the earth. They had been traveling so for twenty minutes and were over wild and rugged mountains when Ram Singh spoke calmly into the phones that connected him with Wentworth.

"There is a light, *sahib*, two points to the right, high in the mountain."

Wentworth peered where Ram Singh had indicated. Vaguely his glasses made out the outlines of a cabin on the hill and spidery above it the triple towers of a beam radio station piercing the night!

"That's fine, Ram Singh," Wentworth said quietly. "No chance to make a landing. I'm going to use a parachute."

He detached the head-phone, climbed on the seat and threw a leg over the side. The night was moonless and low, scattered clouds dotted the skies. Below was a darkness like death. With a wave of his hand, Wentworth sprang off into the abyss, yanked the rip cord. Dimly seen tree branches, upthrust tips of evergreens seemed to leap at him. Then he landed heavily, a leg twisted painfully. He fought to his feet instantly, struggled clear of the 'chute. Limping, he folded and carried the sail a hundred yards away where he cached it in a hollow tree. Swiftly then he stripped off his flying suit, revealing himself clad in breeches and puttees—with a forty-five calibre automatic strapped low on each thigh!

Between the thick trunks of trees, he could make out the yellow glimmer of light in the house he had spotted from the plane. He went directly toward it, feet silent on the thick soft evergreen needles that covered the ground.

The house was about fifteen feet square and built of logs. The window from which the steady white glare of electric lights threw a square shaft of light was on the side nearest him. The beam showed heavy black wires which ran to a smaller house, apparently the power plant, and other wires which slanted off toward three tall radio masts that showed spidery against the sky.

Wentworth stole forward.

He pressed listening against the side of the house. Within, he heard one voice talking sharply. There were pauses in the voice, then more words. Either the person he talked to was speaking too softly to be heard or the speaker was using a telephone. No words penetrated the thick logs, only the rumble of the voice. Wentworth eased toward the window, slipped his cigarette lighter from his pocket and used its side as a mirror to spy on the interior.

A man was nodding his head at the mouthpiece of a wall telephone. Now and then he gestured with his right hand while he held the receiver close to his ear with the left. A quick smile flashed across Wentworth's face. He slid away from the window and circled swiftly to the door.

His searching fingers found a dangling latch string and put slow pressure upon it. Within there was a creak!

Wentworth kicked the door open and sprang in with a gun in his right hand. The man whirled from the phone with a startled exclamation, dropped the receiver and clawed for a knife at his belt.

"No, no!" said Wentworth softly. "Just go on talking. But be careful what you say, *damned careful!*"

HE KICKED the door shut and his alert eyes held the man's gaze. For a long minute the duel of wills continued, then the hand sagged away from the knife handle. The man was young, clad much like Wentworth, in corduroy breeches and khaki shirt. He had an intelligent, pale brow shadowed by a mop of black hair, but a small, weak mouth robbed his face of character.

Wentworth said, "Go on talking, quickly!"

At Wentworth's advance, the man winced, fumbled for the receiver. He sidled up to the phone, eyes fearful.

"Hello," he said weakly.

The receiver made raspy sounds.

"The—the wind blew the door open," he said hurriedly, "and

86

it startled me. Listen, I tell you the beam was going every minute of the time. I can't help it if the plane didn't follow it. All he had to do was look at his compass and… All right, I'll shut it off. Sure, right away."

He groped for the hook with the receiver, eyes fixed on Wentworth.

"A little to the right," said Wentworth.

"Huhn!" the man was startled, then the jerked his eyes to the receiver, said, "Oh," and found the hook. He stood there then.

"Who are you?" he asked once more.

"Detective Sergeant Cohalan of New York," said Wentworth. "You're right about the reason the plane didn't fall into your trap. The pilot believed the compass instead of the radio!"

The man stared at him. "I don't know what you mean," he said woodenly.

Wentworth nodded cheerfully. "Of course not. Better cut off the radio beam. How long before those men will be here?"

"I don't know," the youth said again and reached up and pulled a switch on a black radio control board.

Wentworth inspected the cabin's one room slowly, saw that there were bunks for four men on each side of an iron stove. Wide cleats had been nailed to the wall, forming a ladder. An attic had been made by laying green saplings across the tie beams that bridged the gable roof. As he glanced upward, keeping the gun warily on his prisoner, the saplings vibrated and danced!

They thumped dully in slow time as if someone beat on them with something heavy that he could not swing fast. Wentworth identified the sound readily enough. Some person, probably gagged and bound, was beating his feet to attract attention. He looked quickly back to the man beside the radio control board.

"You and I," he said, "are going upstairs. We want to know what it is that makes that queer noise."

A draft fanned Wentworth's back and he ducked sharply to his right, whirling as he sprang. He brought up heavily with his shoulders against the wall. His back hit the logs and the gun in his right hand blasted. Its report blended with the lighter crash of a pistol from the doorway. The man crouched there had a stunned, surprised look in his eyes. Wentworth's bullet had driven him back against the door jamb, but his gun was still in his hand. He lifted it, and Wentworth fired again, deliberately. The man spun to his left, hit the wall, and slammed down to the floor.

WENTWORTH'S RIGHT gun swiveled and held the radioman, just starting into action with his drawn knife swordwise across his fist. The man straightened slowly, eyes no longer dazed but filled with hating anger, weak lips pulled back from narrow long teeth that were yellow and looked sharp. Wentworth flicked a glance to the man on the floor, then ducked like light itself as swift movement caught the tail of his eye. Steel glinted in a silvery streak toward him. The man had thrown the knife!

The right gun jerked up, but Wentworth did not fire. Instead, he held the weapon leveled on the radio man. Holstering his left gun, he reached up with that hand and plucked the still quivering knife from the wall beside his throat.

"That was a good throw," he said drily, "but you are inexperienced. In knife throwing, you should always remember that your victim is sure to see your throw and dodge. You should aim at a part of the body that he cannot move swiftly—the belly is a good spot."

The youth's hands were clenched at his sides, his yellow sharp teeth still bared.

"Thanks," he said violently. "I hope to have the chance to try that on you."

Wentworth nodded calmly and said, "We're going upstairs."

"I'm not," the knifer declared defiantly.

Wentworth raised his brows and, holstering the gun, tossed the knife to his right hand. He walked straight at the man, moving on his toes, his shoulders rolled forward. The man backed away from him, pace for pace. Wentworth's leap surprised him. In stumbling haste, the man was unable to escape the swift dart of a left hand that caught his shoulder and spun him. The knife pricked his back above the kidney.

The man trembled beneath the knife.

"I have always observed," Wentworth told him pleasantly, "that a man carries generally the weapon he fears most himself. I'm warning you. The first break you make, this little plaything of yours is going to slide right through your kidney. You are doubtless familiar with the effects of that pleasant little thrust?"

The trembling increased. There was no mirth on the heavy, jowled face that Wentworth had built to create the nonexistent Cohalan, but his gray-blue eyes were bright and interested. He kept the knife at his prisoner's back, and side by side they climbed up the wide cleats of the ladder.

When the radio man stepped out upon the saplings, Wentworth reversed the knife and snapped the hilt against the man's head just behind the ear. He tumbled limply down, and through the shadows of the loft Wentworth made out the thin figure of a prostrate man. He crossed to him and removed a tight gag, flashed on the tiny finger of a small flashlight.

The face in the ray of light was pale and lined with more than age, the tousled iron-gray hair was a thick crest.

A smile lighted Wentworth's heavy, disguised face. "Don't tell me you're Jonas Curley!" he exclaimed gaily.

He was busy with the man's bonds, and when the prisoner's hands came free, the man raised one slowly to his throat, twisted his head. He got out hoarse words.

"Yes… Curley," he groaned. "Water!"

This was greater luck than Wentworth could have hoped for. He had found a man who might be able to help identify the leaders, who might have valuable information! The reason for his presence here was obvious. He had been shipped west to apply the principle of his invention to the radio scheme they had devised.

Wentworth told the old man his false identity as Detective Sergeant Cohalan and helped him to the floor below. He put a dipper of water in his trembling hands and climbed swiftly back to the attic where he bound and gagged the radio man, already recovering from the light blow with the knife.

He dropped to the cabin floor again and with swift, efficient energy, he wrecked the radio plant while the old man watched. He knew what to wreck and he did a thorough job. He sent

Jonas Curley out into the night to wait for him then and, jerking the gunman he had killed over on his back, he imprinted on the dead man's forehead the red seal of the Spider's justice.

From a corner, he snatched a length of rope, rigged it over a rafter, noosed it about the dead man's throat and hanged him before the door. He stared mockingly at the corpse as it swung slowly back and forth, rotating in slow, diminishing turns. When the other men returned, they would meet the Spider's justice face to face!

WHEN WENTWORTH slipped out into the night, closing the door, he found old Jonas Curley standing just where he had left him. Taking the aged inventor's bony arm, he led him toward a hiding place. The old man moved with the shambling feet and sagging shoulders of one without hope. When Wentworth placed him in a clump of shrubbery, he sat down dejectedly, flat on the earth, and leaned weakly against a dead log.

"My daughter and my granddaughter?" he croaked, his throat still hoarse from the gag. "My little Nellie? Have—have you—"

Wentworth stood staring down at the thin old man barely visible in the shadows. He had good reason to think that Curley's "little Nellie" was a willing ally of the Pirates.

"Your daughter is safe at home, Mr. Curley," he said slowly, "but so far, we haven't been able to find your granddaughter, Nellie."

The old man's head sagged even lower.

"No, no!" his voice shook. "Of course, you haven't found her! Why did you have to interfere? Why couldn't you let them have my invention so that little Nellie could come back to me?"

91

Wentworth frowned. Was it possible that Curley didn't know to what use his invention was being put? If that were true, the Spider could get no help from the old inventor.

"Do you think my invention matters if I do not find my little Nell? What do I care about money?" His words were a worn complaint. "Old Jonas Curley has lived all these years in poverty. A few more mean nothing to me. But Nell—" He moaned and something like a sob shook the bent shoulders.

"Did you know," Wentworth asked quietly, "that your invention is being used to kill thousands of people, Mr. Curley? That your transformer is being used to loot trains and planes of millions of dollars in cash, to kill people so that their bodies can be stripped of valuables?"

Wentworth explained in detail then what had happened, how the invention was being used. There was silence between the two men when he had finished, silence broken only by the sighing of wind. Finally, Curley spoke.

"And my little Nell is in the hands of fiends like that!" he groaned.

Wentworth shook his head. The aged inventor was too absorbed in his granddaughter and her fate for any other thing to penetrate his thoughts. The death of thousands, the loot of millions, these were as nothing beside the fact that his granddaughter was in the criminals' hands.

Wentworth frowned in the darkness. It was hard for the Spider to conceive of such an attitude, he who time and again had chosen between duty and the death of his loved ones, and chosen always that the loved one should face death rather than that humanity should suffer.

Wentworth spoke sharply. "You had better remain here quietly. I am going to explore a little and soon, I think, other men will come. I must be ready for them."

He slipped away through the darkness, circled the cabin and found a path which, after half a mile, led to a small, level field. In the edge of the forest, a plane had been covered with tree limbs to hide it from above. He yanked open the cowling and removed the ignition wires, thrusting them into his pocket. He hurried back to Curley then.

"There's an air field along a path out back," Wentworth told him. "Follow that path until you reach the field, then hide in the bushes to the right. I'll be along presently."

The old man raised his gaunt height slowly from the shrubbery. He stared at Wentworth and said hesitantly, "I'm afraid. Why must I go alone? What are you going to do?"

Wentworth laughed softly.

"I'm going to wait for the other men to return," he said. "There can't be more than six or eight of them...."

CHAPTER 11
A CORPSE CRAWLS

ALONE, WENTWORTH slipped to the door of the house. There was a step there made of logs held in place by stakes driven into the earth.

From the tool kit he carried always beneath his arm, Wentworth pulled out a tight ball of silken cord. It was a little smaller than a pencil and, made of the highest quality, triple-twisted silk, would stand a strain of seven hundred pounds. It was the cord which police and newspapers, when bits of it were found, called the Spider's Web. Wentworth looped it over one of the stakes beside the step and carried the two ends off into the darkness, then he slipped back to the cover of trees and shrubbery that commanded the cabin door.

There he removed his shirt and draped it over low shrubs in front of the spot where he sat and settled down to wait. The needles of the pines made him a soft cushion and he rested his back against the bole of a tree.

There was more than mere vengeance behind Wentworth's plan. He doubted that lesser members of the gang would know the hiding place of Captain Kidd, and he knew that the chief of this particular post must be with the men who had been waiting to strip the plane of its wealth. The radio man's tone over the phone told him that. Wentworth wanted to take that leader alive and force him to betray the Pirates' secrets!

For half an hour, Wentworth sat waiting before he caught the first warning of men's approach. It was the click of a horseshoe on stone and it drifted up from the valley behind him. That was all until he caught the rumble of a man's distant voice vibrating briefly through the night and, a short while later, the soft thudding of hoofs on yielding earth.

Wentworth watched the dark, bunched forms against the sky as, saddle leather creaking, horses blowing, the riders came out of the woods. Men grumbled words at each other and swung down.

"Bill, stay with the horses," a man ordered, but which man spoke, which was the leader, Wentworth could not discern.

The men stumped toward the cabin in a close group. Hands fumbled with the door, then the light from within tunneled out into the blackness and a man cried out hoarsely and another cursed once in a high startled voice. The dead man, hanging in his noose, swayed gently back and forth, turning slowly to the right, deliberately back to the left again. The wound in his side had stained his shirt and the red seal on his forehead gleamed.

"The Spider!"

"TO COVER, all of you!" a harsh voice barked, and one man shorter than the rest, shorter, but broad as the doorway, stood for an instant clear in the lighted doorway, pointing hiding places and spots to search.

Wentworth grinned in the darkness and raised one of his guns. His purpose was accomplished, he knew the leader now. Deliberately Wentworth drew a bead and squeezed the trigger.

At the crash, the leader flung prostrate and rolled to cover within the cabin. The corpse, the rope severed cleanly by Wentworth's bullet, plopped ludicrously to the floor. When the last echo of that single shot had clapped back from the hills, when the crash of spluttering pistol fire that had answered died out, Wentworth sent through the night the mocking flat laughter of the Spider! It was not loud, yet its sibilance carried clearly to every man crouched in the darkness about the cabin.

"*Death!*" Wentworth chanted. "*The Spider brings death!*"

Hysterical shots answered. Wentworth selected the one nearest the panicky horses rearing off to his right and fired deliberately. A man screamed and that gun did not fire again. Once more Wentworth sent his chilling laughter through the gloom. The horses whinnied, reared, crashed off into the shrubbery. Their hoofbeats dwindled into the thick night.

Wentworth had long schooled himself to fire without aim, to fire by the feel of his guns as a man points his finger accurately in the darkness. And when he shot, it was through the shirt draped before him. The powder flare scorched his shirt, but though its flash spread a brief lurid glow in the darkness, it made no spearpoint of flame to guide the gangsters' bullets.

Twice more Wentworth's careful shots sped into the night, and twice more guns were silenced. Only three men were left now—and one of those was hiding in the cabin—but the lead of the two who still fired was nipping dangerously close to where the Spider hid. They had located his ambush and the shrubbery cracked with their whining lead.

It was time for the Spider to use the other trick for which he had paved the way when he had looped that length of silk cord about a stake by the doorstep. On his belly, Wentworth wormed from his shrub-masked lair. He found the ends of the cord where he had fastened them to a bush, then wormed on toward where the first man had screamed with the Spider's bullet in his vitals.

When he had found the corpse, he printed his seal on the man's forehead, then about his throat he fastened one end of the silken cord that led to the door. He wrapped the other end of the line about his forearm and, feet braced against a tree, put his weight and strength into a slow, steady tug.

The body inched forward across the earth, creeping toward the door of the cabin, crawling like a stealthy murderer with his belly on the ground! After each heave of the cord, Wentworth's lips twisted in a mocking grim smile.

Set a crook to catch a crook, a corpse to make more corpses! Wentworth's lips twisted in a mocking smile. After each heave of the cord, he straightened and waited, peering at the dark trees where his two enemies still hid. In his right hand he grasped his automatic, a handkerchief bound across its muzzle to mask its powder flash.

Slowly, with no more sound than a snake might make, he dragged the body across the earth toward the cabin. It caught on a shrub at the edge of the glow from the door, jerked loose with a quivering of branches and slid into the half-light. Guns spat from two separate points in the bushes, one almost beside the spot where Wentworth had hidden. He fired twice in swift succession. Something floundered and crashed in the underbrush. A man was in the throes of death. Then silence, and no more lead whined toward him.

A SLOW smile twisted Wentworth's lips. Of six men who had come, one remained alive, the leader. That was as he wished it. He slid then toward the body he had used as a decoy. He picked it up, edged to the cabin door and let the body's head sag forward as if a man peered inside. No shot, no sound came from within.

Wentworth darted to the window. It was open, and, peering

in cautiously, he found no trace of the dwarf-like leader. He whirled and raced toward the air field. After a quarter mile sprint, he cut soft-footed into the woods.

Undoubtedly the leader had found the plane crippled and, by now, had doubled back to lie in ambush. If Wentworth could reach Curley, he might get some clue to the gang leader's whereabouts.

He advanced cautiously until the lighter darkness of the clearing showed through the black stripes of the tree trunks, then called softly: "Curley! It's Cohalan. Where are you?"

He called twice before he heard a faint response thirty feet to his right. Cautiously, he made a circuit of the spot. It took fifteen minutes and Curley called questioningly. The voice startled Wentworth with its closeness, but he did not answer. He lay flat on his belly and wormed toward that voice. He got his gun ready in his right hand, gripped the pencil ray firmly in his left—and heard a hoarse whisper within arm's length.

"Call again!" it ordered. The voice could not have carried more than five feet.

Wentworth smiled thinly. But for his perpetual caution, the Spider would have walked into this simple trap set by the leader of the Pirate gang. Obviously the man had found old Curley and used him to lay an ambush. Easy enough for the Spider to kill this man, but he must be captured alive. Wentworth got to his feet, squeezed on the light—then hurled himself frantically to one side. A gun blasted at him from the darkness and the pirate's lead whined past within an inch of the Spider's side!

Wentworth cried out horribly and thrashed the underbrush

with his left hand. But even as he screamed, he leaped a clear six feet to one side, landing silently on his toes, gun reversed in his hand. When once more the other's pistol smashed lead into the night, Wentworth sprang forward and whipped down violently with his automatic.

A deep voice groaned and cursed and Wentworth heard the pirate's gun thud to the ground. He jerked up his weapon to strike again, but a fist caught him low in the body and pain streaked like tearing claws through his loins. He hit the ground and a heavy boot crashed against his side. Then, thunderously, a gun bellowed and a terrific weight slammed down across his shoulders. Dimly, Wentworth heard a cracked voice shouting.

"Damn you!" it howled. *"Damn you!"*

HE REALIZED vaguely that this was Jonas Curley's voice, Jonas Curley crying curses into the black night. Something warm and liquid was flowing over his back. Blood. Curley had shot the pirate!

Even through his pain, Wentworth felt that thought thudding, and it brought despair. He had risked his life in a dozen different ways to take this man alive, to seize a leader of the Pirates who could give him a clue to the dread Captain Kidd. And now that man lay inert upon his back and his blood dribbled down upon the Spider....

There was a chance the man had been only wounded... Feverishly Wentworth fought clear of that body.

Curley's curses ceased and Wentworth felt the tug of the inventor's feeble strength on the body that pinned him to the earth. Clear at last, he fumbled out matches.

The man he had risked death six times over to capture alive, now lay upon the ground with the back of his head blown off!

Wentworth shook out the match and got limply to his feet. He found Curley's hand, recovered his gun.

"You saved my life, Curley," he said. "I won't forget it."

He said nothing of his loss, of the fact that now the leader was slain, they would have no one to lead them to the headquarters of the gang. He still had the radio man bound in the loft of the cabin, but it was doubtful if anyone less than the leader knew how to reach Captain Kidd.

Wentworth led Curley rapidly to the cabin again. As he passed the window, he heard a voice say shrilly, "I still hear shooting and I don't know what's happened to the plane."

Wentworth reached the door in a stride. The radio man whirled and sprang to the attack. Wentworth caught him in mid-leap with a punch that floored him. A knife slithered from his hand and Wentworth grinned.

"Naughty, naughty," he said, "don't you ever learn anything?"

After a moment's struggle, he bound the pirate's wrists, then spun him toward the doorway. Curley stood there, face lowering with anger. He stooped and picked up the knife.

"Shall I kill this rat, too?" he asked. "His name is Howard Katz. I befriended him once and taught him electricity."

Wentworth laughed abruptly, pivoted toward the door.

"Not yet, Curley," he said. "We'll make him talk first—in New York. They have a way with crooks there."

Wentworth stalked off into the darkness while Curley followed with the prisoner and the knife. Katz punctuated the walk to the plane with repeated cries and when they were ready to leave, the ignition wires replaced and the motor warming up, Wentworth found the man's back was bloody from the knife point.

He stared at Curley in the light of the plane's landing lights and the inventor met his questioning gaze grimly.

"I don't believe he does know where the headquarters are," he said. "Shall we kill him now?"

Hard amusement lurked in Wentworth's eyes.

"Wouldn't you rather be burned for it?" he inquired.

Curley seized Katz's throat with his left hand, pricked his belly with the knife.

Katz moaned and collapsed. He tossed on the ground in an agony of fear.

"Oh, God," he groaned. "Don't leave me here! Take me to a hospital! I'll talk. *God, I'll talk!*"

"**GO AHEAD,**" Wentworth ordered. "Where can we find Captain Kidd?"

"If I talk now, you'll leave me," Katz whined. "I won't talk until we get to a hospital, to New York. Captain Kidd's in New York."

Wentworth pounded at the man in vain. "I'll tell you when I get to a hospital," he insisted, "and not before."

Wentworth stared at the man grimly. Hope was thrilling within him. A chance of victory had been snatched from the maw of defeat. He whirled toward the inventor and saw that Curley's eyes were dazed.

"What's the matter?" Wentworth demanded quickly.

The old man shook his head heavily. "Captain Kidd," he muttered. "So that's it?"

Wentworth frowned. "If you know anything, spill it," he ordered sharply.

"I don't know a thing," Curley said.

Wentworth stared at him a moment longer, then shrugged and yanked Katz to his feet. There wasn't time to delay. The old inventor was probably suffering from the reaction of his violence. Wentworth strapped Katz in the forward cockpit beside Curley and climbed in behind. He shot the plane deftly clear of encroaching trees and flew back to New York like a demon, braving the dwindling gasoline supply to avoid stops. Within minutes now, he would have Katz in a hospital. He would force the man to reveal where Captain Kidd had headquarters—and the avenging Spider would strike!

He dropped the plane almost dead in a three-point landing, rolling scarcely fifty feet, sprang to the wing and reached in to unstrap the man who would lead the Spider to victory. The man was limp.

As Wentworth touched him, he felt the flesh cold and clammy beneath his hands. A more cruel cold stabbed at Wentworth's heart. Good God, was it possible, that after all these hours of sleepless travail, these hours of battle and risk of death in the mountain wilds, was it possible that on the brink of victory....

He groped for Katz's pulse, then lifted his hands from the futile task and stared, grim-eyed into Curley's face.

"Katz is dead," he said coldly. "Why did you kill him?"

CHAPTER 12
THE SPIDER TURNS FLY

WENTWORTH FELT wrath surge up within him to battle with the cold pain of defeat. He could see now that one of those knife wounds in Katz's body had been deeper than a prick, could see that the man who was to lead him to victory had bled to death from one of those small, torturing slashes.

"I—I just found it out," Curley stammered, "just a few minutes ago. I tried to make him talk to save time when we landed, and... Do you want to arrest me?"

Wentworth's direct stare seemed to disconcert the aged inventor so that his head bowed beneath his bushy crest of gray white hair. The Spider was thinking swiftly. Because of this man he had rescued from the Pirates, he had been balked within minutes of triumph. His mind raced back to Curley's killing of the pirate leader, to his strange behavior at the mention of Captain Kidd's name, considered his murder of Harry Katz. Was it possible the inventor, instead of being a victim of the Pirates, actually was a leader in the gangs? Perhaps he had quarreled with some element among the Pirates and for that reason had been bound.

"Do you want to arrest me?" the old man quavered again. "This is twice now that I have killed the man you wanted to lead you to the Pirates."

Wentworth shook his head slowly. "No, I don't want to arrest you," he said. "When we have crossed to New York, I want you

103

to go to headquarters for a few moments, then you can do as you wish."

Curious people were thronging about now, airport attendants with curious eyes on the bloodstained, bullet-torn shirt that Wentworth wore, staring at the dead man sagging in the cockpit. Wentworth's false identity as a detective sergeant dispensed with ceremonies, however, and he was able to take the inventor directly to Kirkpatrick's office.

He signaled that Curley was to be released and a shadow was immediately put on his trail.

Wentworth then told Kirkpatrick the results of his trip and urged an immediate warning to all pilots to watch their compasses closely and steer by them, rather than by the radio beam.

"Whenever a discrepancy in the beam is found," Wentworth said crisply, "the spot of the occurrence should be marked and other planes should immediately follow the indicated trail and destroy the stations found. If fighting planes could follow each mail plane, it would be speedier."

Kirkpatrick had nothing of value to report. There was no trace of Curley's granddaughter. No one had molested the daughter who had gone away to visit relatives. But a silk train had been stripped of its valuable cargo in an incredibly brazen holdup in Chicago.

"People have stopped riding trains," Kirkpatrick said crisply. "Buses and autos jam the roads and I'm afraid the Pirates will strike at those any night now. Running pilot engines with soldiers aboard does no good. It only adds to the dead.

"An hour ago, I received word that the Green Fire was turned on an apartment house here. The first flash killed a great number, all who happened to be near light sockets or touching metal. Then the Pirates went through the house systematically and killed people as they looted."

Wentworth asked grimly, "There were knife wounds on the people?"

"You guessed it," Kirkpatrick told him. "The knife wounds were cauterized and apparently death occurred from electrocution rather than the stab."

Silence fell between the two friends. Wentworth leaned forward, head on his hands. This trail of Curley might lead to some tangible clue, but aside from that or accidental contact, there was little to work on. The police were doing the best they could, but their usual methods of attack seemed useless.

Apparently, the Pirates had embraced most of the criminal world in their slashing, lightning attacks. The stool pigeons on whom the police relied so largely for their information either were themselves involved or intimidated.

Wentworth lifted his head. A bitterness of depression was upon him. He was physically weary, his brain was fagged from hours of battle with scant sleep, from hours of struggling with the problem. He stared past Kirkpatrick and saw through the high, dusty windows the first flaring dance of Neon advertising signs that heralded the night. As he watched, the street lights blinked on gaily.

But if they were gay, they were the only lively things about the city. No theatre-going crowds swelled the streets, no lines of sleek, youth-filled cars crowded the traffic lanes. It was if

New York felt a doom upon it, a doom of death and mysterious ghoulish pillagings.

Wentworth got slowly to his feet, stood staring out the window with a tight smile playing about his strong mouth. There was only one course left, one course that would stop the Pirates before the country was completely at their mercy. He must offer himself as bait in a trap for Captain Kidd. The Spider would play the fly—the fly with a sting!

AN HOUR later, immaculate in the formal evening dress he wore so well, he dropped from a taxi at the entrance to *Chez François*, where he was to meet Nita and young Jim Walsh. In the act of paying off the cab driver, he stiffened, staring at the tense white face of a woman in a taxi that flashed past, with a crashing of gears, gathering speed swiftly. It was Nita!

Wentworth sprang back into the cab.

"Follow that red taxi!" he ordered sharply, and the size of the bill he thrust into the driver's hand overcame the man's vocal scruples against pursuit. The motor drummed into swift, powerful action.

Wentworth sat alertly forward in his seat, watching the cab ahead. Within five blocks, he located the car that Nita was pursuing, a cream-colored taxi that flashed chromium plating at each street light. He sank back watchfully on the cushions. He knew of only one thing that could draw Nita from the rendezvous. She must have seen either Nellie Curley, the girl all the city's police hunted, or she had seen the gangster Dutch Brogard, with whom the girl was known to associate. A slow smile twitched Wentworth's mouth corners. Were the Pirates already setting their trap for the Spider, through Nita?

It seemed probable. The fact that Nita must have seen either Nellie Curley or Dutch Brogard in *Chez François* indicated that. After all, Richard Wentworth was a man of some fame. The fact that he frequented *Chez François* would be easily discovered by anyone who, like Captain Kidd, had taken the trouble to investigate him. She would not have allowed either the girl or Dutch to visit the night club unless it was part of some prearranged plan, *unless she wanted the Spider to see and follow them!*

Yes, Wentworth was positive that the gangsters were setting a trap. His smile turned grim and hard. Well, the Spider was spinning a web, too! An abrupt fear brought a deep vertical crease between his brows. But suppose this were not a trap; suppose Nita had not been expected to follow and those ruthless killers should attack Nita!

He cursed under his breath, touched the gun beneath his arm. He must protect Nita… Yet if it was the trap he expected, he would ruin all his chances by crowding too close to that taxi ahead. He must take the chance, risk dear Nita's life… He sat tensely while the taxi ahead zig-zagged eastward across the town, sped north on Fifth Avenue. Nita finally alighted before an apartment house and Wentworth jumped out a half block away and dismissed his own cab.

"Return to your stand," he ordered. "In a short while a Lancia should arrive with a Hindu chauffeur. Tell him just what happened and where you left me." Ram Singh was due momentarily to return from the West and Wentworth had left orders that the faithful Hindu was to follow to the night club.

"Sure, captain," the driver saluted Wentworth. "I'll do that, and any time you get tired of a foreigner for a chauffeur, me name's Shamus O'Hara."

Wentworth said, "Thanks, O'Hara. Give the Hindu your name and address."

He turned and strolled up the street, tapping his cane softly. When her cab had gone, Nita hurried up Fifth Avenue and spoke swiftly to the *chasseur* at a building three doors away. Sauntering closer, Wentworth saw three men come out of the softly lighted doorway.

They tipped their hats and Nita and the three went back into the apartment building.

After a moment Wentworth strolled in also. A hall boy stepped forward and Wentworth, reasoning swiftly, asked for the apartment of Nellie Curley's gangster friend, Dutch Brogard. The hall-boy reached for the house phone.

"Never mind," said Wentworth casually, "I'm expected. Will you just take me up?"

The boy hesitated. Wentworth had some money in his hand. The boy smiled widely, bowed, and marched to the elevator. The money changed hands and Wentworth went swiftly upward.

At the entrance of the gangster's apartment Wentworth deftly used a lock-pick from the compact tool kit beneath his arm and, in less than a minute, the bolt clicked smoothly back. He eased open the door.

Sound reached him then, a muffled sound of horrible pain,

of a woman suffering! And, God above! That most terrifying of odors, the odor that before this had set nausea twitching in his body, cloyed his nostrils, the scent of burning flesh! With a cry of *Nita!* that he choked in his throat, Wentworth flung into the apartment.

HE TOOK two strides down a darkened hall whose end was draped with curtains. But as he sprang toward them, the curtains were snatched aside and a heavy man with a gun in his hand stared into his face. Wentworth's left hand closed on the man's gun wrist and wrenched it aside. His right fist slammed up like a pile-driver and hammered the man backward into the room.

Wentworth went in behind him, gun in hand. There were two other persons in the room, but both were flat upon their backs, strained across a bed with arms and feet tied together. One was a man; the other a woman, a girl with glorious blonde hair, a girl naked to the waist with her torn scarlet dress in rags about her!

The man lay beside her and his dress shirt had been ripped open to the waist. Upon the body of each, upon the man's hairy, muscled chest, upon the girls' young and tender breasts, had been carved with searing iron, the flag of the Pirates! These two had been executed by Captain Kidd!

He knew the man. He was Dutch Brogard, the gangster! And the girl, the girl was the granddaughter of Jonas Curley, little Nell, for whom the police of the whole city had been searching!

The Spider stared down at their bodies, realizing that here *all* his theories crumpled. If Jonas Curley were one of the Pirates, why had first his grandson, and now the granddaughter, whom it was obvious he loved even above his own life, been slain so horribly? Her appearance at the night club proved at least that she had not been kidnapped. But there was no time to speculate. Nita had come into this building, and... Wentworth whirled and raced through the other rooms of the apartment. But there was no trace of Nita, or of the three men who had come with her!

He pounded back to the room where the two lay dead and for the first time examined the man he had knocked out on entering. It was Ralph Donaghue, the fat private detective with whom Wentworth had tangled twice before on the trail of the Pirates!

Even now, the detective was muttering and stirring with returning consciousness. But Wentworth had no time to investigate him. Nita had walked into this building and disappeared. Perhaps, even now, in some oilier apartment, those fiends of Captain Kidd were inflicting upon her the torture of the skull and crossbones flag....

With a curse that was half a prayer, Wentworth strode from the apartment, collared the hall-boy.

"A woman in a white evening dress and three men came in just ahead of me," he said rapidly. "Where did they go?"

The boy stared at Wentworth, then pointed.

Wentworth cursed. The building had a second exit on the side street. The three men had taken Nita straight through the lobby and away again! He had lost fifteen minutes.

He raced to the street. But not before he had given the hall-boy a brief message for Ram Singh. In the cab rank, Wentworth found the driver who had carried Nita and the gangsters away and, in ten minutes, he alighted a block from the address to which they had gone. It was a squalid tenement on a dark and deserted street.

He moved briskly along, tapping his cane, and passed the doorway Nita had entered without a glance, though his heart raced with fear for her. The corners of his eyes saw that the door stood open, that the hall within was a black pocket of shadows. He turned the next corner. A dilapidated fence was beside him now. He thrust his cane through a suspender strap, caught the top of the fence with both hands and vaulted over cleanly, dropping into darkness.

FOR A full two minutes he crouched there, waiting. There was no sound, no movement. He drifted like a shadow across the yard, squirmed through a broken plank into the next and turned toward the house. The next building was the one Nita had entered. Up through the house he worked his slow way, past hot, rancid rooms, through the rank, clinging odors of greasy cooking. He dislodged the roof scuttle with his cane and pulled himself up to the roof. On silent feet, he crossed to the gang house, found the scuttle there, unfastened and opened it. But, on the point of dropping into the darkness below, he hesitated.

It was all ridiculously easy. Too easy. Even the least intelligent of crooks attempting the abduction of the Spider's beloved would take more precautions against attack. And that obvious tracing of her through the taxi driver. Yes, too easy. Was it only that he had acted with more speed than they expected?

Wentworth crouched at the scuttle and listened. Within all was silence. Hot air gusted up from within, bringing familiar tenement odors. He cursed beneath his breath. Was the Spider developing a case of nerves that he saw peril even in silence and deserted streets?

With a shrug of his shoulders, Wentworth slipped a black mask over his eyes, and lowered himself into the house, dangling at arm length. Instantly the place was bathed in brilliant light. Across the gravel roof above, feet pounded.

Though blinded by the light, Wentworth acted swiftly. He dropped to the floor, dived, and rolled with guns flashing to his hands. As he rolled, his eyes swept about him. There was no one in the room!

He came swiftly to his feet, crouching. The roof scuttle thudded into place. He pitched two swift shots through it and heard a weight thump down on it. He smiled thinly. The Spider had scored first blood! In a stride, he reached the door, yanked at the knob. It came off in his hand, and then—seemingly within the room—*a woman laughed!*

Wentworth whirled at the door, but his guns found no target.

"No, dear Spider," the woman's voice said sibilantly, "you can't find me. I'm not in the room, but I can see you and hear you. And you can hear me!"

Wentworth spotted a small loudspeaker attachment in a corner. The voice came from that. There were slots in the walls, a half dozen of them commanding every inch of the room. They looked like loopholes in an armored car, the loopholes through which guns spoke!

"You walked into the trap very nicely, Spider," the woman's voice went on softly. "There were three rooms like this waiting for you here. But this is the strongest. It was nice of you to drop into our strongest trap. In a few minutes, Spider, you die!"

CHAPTER 13
SURRENDER—OR NITA DIES!

WENTWORTH SAW that the light came from two dazzling bulbs in the ceiling, that the one window was covered with a steel plate bolted to the wall. He straightened, smiling.

"I must compliment you—and myself," he said calmly. "Captain Kidd, you have done a thorough job. I appreciate the compliment such preparations pay to the fear you hold for the Spider. You do well to fear me."

The woman's voice rasped. "You merely annoy me."

Wentworth's smile grew taunting. "I could not expect you to acknowledge fear in the presence of your underlings," he said, "but the fact that you dare not face me except from behind walls is proof enough. *You are afraid!*"

For a moment there was silence. When the answer came finally, it was laughter.

"No, no, Spider," said the woman. "You shall have no chance to escape by luring me into the room. You shall die where you are!"

113

Wentworth's two guns swiveled upward and at their crash darkness clapped down upon the room. One trick had failed, but he had others. Swiftly he holstered his weapons, snatched two small phials from the kit that was strapped as always beneath his arm. Beyond the walls he heard shouting. Lights gleamed at the slits in the walls and narrow rays filtered into the darkness where he crouched.

Wentworth dodged them and strode to the door, poured a mixture of fluids from the two phials into the crack by the lock, dribbled some down the woodwork. He flicked flame to his lighter, hiding it beneath his coat, and touched it to the trail of liquid. Then he huddled in a corner.

Blue flame flickered up the door. A terrific blast and Wentworth was up instantly, guns in hand. Dim light came now from the hall. The explosives had blown the door from its hinges. Wentworth plunged into the hall, but he did not race down the stairs. The lights came from there. He raced forward to where the beams fanning up the stairway would outline any figure that moved. He crouched and waited.

He must escape from here, find Nita and blow these Pirates off the earth. Captain Kidd was here. He had heard her voice… Shouts echoed through the house. A door flung open on his left and two men darted out with drawn guns. Wentworth fired twice and they spilled to the floor. One screamed and threshed a moment. The other merely collapsed.

The shouting leaped to a new crescendo. Wentworth took the time, his face lighted by a mocking smile, to brand the two

Wentworth's bullet smashed the microphone just as Bolo shouted "Ten!"

he had slain with his seal, then he tossed their bodies into the open stair well. Shots and yells made a bedlam below.

The Spider darted into the room the two men had come out of. It was empty. In a stride, he crossed to a window that opened on the street. The canyon below was empty, and yet, with this noise, crowds should have swirled there! An auto turned a corner, cruising slowly with its headlights bright, a spot flashing over the walks. It swung lazily left, spurted and within a moment was circling into view again.

During the interval of its absence, five other such cars came into view about the contiguous blocks, including that in which Wentworth was located. He whistled softly. Good Lord, what a trap he had entered! No need to wonder what those cars were. He knew that they were loaded with gunmen and that those men sought just one thing—a glimpse of the Spider!

WENTWORTH LEANED farther from the window, peering up and down the streets. As far as he could see in either direction, that deadly patrol went on. Captain Kidd must have organized the entire Underworld to rid itself once and for all of the Spider! There would be no difficulty in enlisting thousands in such a battle. All had reason to fear the Spider. No crime was too small, but that his all-seeing eyes might pick it out for redress. These men feared the touch of his small red seal to their foreheads as they feared no hell itself. But their very fear would make them the more willing to enlist in an army bent alone on his destruction!

And if they succeeded, what mad looting, what wholesale destruction and murder would sweep the country! This army

116

of crooks, once united, would be almost impossible to suppress. Which meant just one thing—the Spider must survive and smash this gigantic octopus of crime.

But how long could they continue such a patrol against the vigilance of police? The answer came almost as it brushed Wentworth's mind. No such vast organization of criminals need fear a lone patrol car. It could be wiped out by a single coughing blast from a machine gun. And within a minute, six of the gang cars could converge on anyone spot. Nothing less than a wholesale turning out of the police reserves from a half dozen precincts could break that ceaseless cordon!

But already he had delayed too long. He crossed to the door, jammed it shut with a steel wedge from his kit, a thin instrument with teeth set at an angle which, thrust into the crack of the door, would hold it more solidly than any lock. Back at the window, he looped a strand of his thin silken "web" over the casement itself and, twisting the dangling double cord several times about leg and arm, permitted himself to slip down the face of the building.

If one of those questing spotlights turned its ray upward, he would be lost, a swaying black blur against the brick facade like a spider dangling from its thin skein. He slipped slowly to the line of the window below and peered into the room. It was empty and dark. Swiftly, he slid up the casement, eased in. Through the doorway beyond, he could make out lights and swift, whispering movement. He drew in the cord. It was doubled and it was merely necessary to pull on one end to recover it.

He thrust the silk into the tail of his coat and cat-footed across the room, revolver in hand.

Two men were crouched out of range of the steps with a machine gun ready when the Spider should essay the descent!

Wentworth reversed his gun in his hand. He crouched and dived headfirst for the men in the shadows! One straightened with a cry, throwing his pistol about. He was too slow. The butt of the Spider's automatic caught him between the eyes. As they went down together, Wentworth flung his left arm about the machine gunner's throat, holding it in the crook of his elbow. He struck again and that man collapsed, too. He thrust the two out of sight in the room at whose entrance they had crouched, as a cautious voice called from the rear hall.

"What's the matter?"

Wentworth grumbled, "Keep quiet, will you?"

Whispers made a sibilant noise back there in the shadows. Wentworth rapidly stripped off his coat and stiff shirt, drew on the coat and cap of one of the men he had knocked out. Then, half-erect, head down and with the machine gun in his hands, he crept back down the hall, making no effort at concealment.

"Stay where you are," a voice ordered angrily.

"Not me," Wentworth grumbled. "That fool back there gave us away, and—" He could make out now the men who waited there at the back of the hall. There were two of them and they had a machine gun!

"God!" one gulped. "It's not Bill, it's—"

Wentworth squeezed the machine gun's trigger and streamed hot lead into the two crouched there. Even as they crumpled, he vaulted the railing and dropped to the steps below, straddled the banister and slid downward, face foremost, spraying the black shadows below with deadly bullets.

Half way down he braked to a halt with his knees and leaped to the lower hall, throwing himself instantly flat. The questing spotlight of a passing gang car thrust its narrow ray into the open front door. Wentworth saw two men prone on the floor, their hands thrown wide, mute testimony of the fearfulness of the Spider's gunfire.

He was within a few feet of the open, of escape from the trap. His swift and deadly lead, his fertile brain could devise a way out for him, a way to smash even through the cordon of all crookdom. But he made no move toward that yawning door. Instead he moved stealthily toward the rear. The Spider would stay with the battle to the finish. He would rescue Nita in spite of a thousand such gangsters as hemmed him now.

He must find Nita. And where she was, he would find Captain Kidd also, and the other leaders of the gang. Nita had entered this building. Reason told him she would not have been kept on one of the two upper floors once the Spider was located there. But she might be on this floor or in the basement… the basement! That would be the safest, most logical prison. He darted for the back stairway.

But even as Wentworth reached the kitchen door, he halted, transfixed by a booming voice.

"Spider!" it called. "Surrender, or Nita dies!"

WENTWORTH STOOD rigid, teeth bared in an ugly snarl. He had wondered how long it would be before they struck on that device. They knew he was on the premises now, knew that he had not yet escaped from the house, knew that they held a fearful weapon over him, Nita's life!

"Spider," the voice called again. "Surrender or Nita dies!"

Wentworth ground out a curse.

The voice boomed on:

"You cannot escape, Spider. Even if you get out of this building, the streets for a mile around are filled with gunmen waiting for you. Every person who moves on those streets is to be shot down instantly. If you move there, a dozen guns will pour lead into your body.

"Surrender, Spider, or *Nita will be made to walk into the streets in your place!*"

Wentworth was slipping up the hall now, red rage burning in his heart. Fiends, they were, but wise. They were right. He would surrender to save Nita's life. Even while he flayed himself for such a decision, he knew that he would do it. This was no issue of humanity or Nita. It was her life against his surrender. And the gangster who took the Spider prisoner might live—briefly—to regret that capture!

Abruptly, he froze in his tracks. Surely, that voice came from behind this door to his right. With breath caught in his throat, a triumphant gleam in his eyes, Wentworth sprang to the door. But, hand on knob, he hesitated. Three traps, the woman had said, and her voice had sounded in that trap above without her presence in the room. This might be another of her traps.

Wentworth crouched behind the protection of the wall, flung the door wide and snapped his hand to cover.

Instantly, light blazed out from within, bathing the hall in brilliant white. A machine gun cackled and lead carved a pattern on the hallway wall. But Wentworth was clear. He cursed softly. Trap Number Two had been sprung futilely. When the gun chatter died, the voice boomed again.

"You cannot find me, Spider. Give up. Come up the stairs with your hands in the air, or Nita will be forced to walk where the bullets can find her! You have ten seconds. I will count. *One....*"

Wentworth's breath was harsh in his throat. Ten seconds before they sent Nita to her death. What choice did he have but to walk up those steps with his hands high above his head—walk probably into the muzzle of a machine gun spitting death!

"Two!" boomed the voice.

Wentworth jerked his head about, staring toward the darkness of the steps. That was where they wanted him to walk, *yet he had killed every man on those two upper floors!*

Wentworth cursed softly. Why hadn't he thought of it before? The woman had boasted she could see him, yet he had blasted his way clear and spread death aloft and he had not found the woman.

He reached the back door even as the radio-conducted voice of the man boomed *"Three!"* He bounded out, ducked to the left, scrambled over the fence and reached the house next to the one in which the traps had been set.

Dimly he heard the voice rasping *"Four!"*

He had six seconds then, six seconds to battle for Nita's life.

What a pitifully small time out of all eternity to battle for the one being who meant everything to him!

"Five!" boomed the voice, as unhurrying, but as inexorable, as time itself.

He found the back door of the house next door open and slipped in, stole along the hall toward the front of the building.

"Six!" The voice came still from the house next door, booming through the halls. "Six, Spider. Four seconds to go. If you don't show yourself, Nita walks into the streets. The word *ten* will signal her death!"

Wentworth's teeth locked tightly, he took the steps in long, silent leaps, whirled backward into the hall at the second floor, spurted to the third.

"Nine!" he heard the voice. One second of life for Nita, one second! Wentworth gasped a prayer, but it was a prayer of thankfulness. For now the voice no longer came from the next house, it came from the room behind the door where he stood!

"One more second, Spider," the voice intoned. "One second. Come up the stairs with your hands in the air, Spider, or—" mocking, hateful laughter then, *"or Nita dies!"*

With a shout of rage that tore his throat, Wentworth kicked open the door, an automatic in each hand. Two persons were in the room, a woman and a man. A heavy, whiskered man sat before a microphone, his face cracked in a satanic grin. The woman stood beside him, and the woman was Captain Kidd!

But Nita! Dear God, *Nita was not in the room!*

If he threw down his guns and surrendered, he still might spare Nita's life. If he threw down his guns....

122

CHAPTER 14
THE THIRD TRAP

THE GUN in Wentworth's right hand and Captain Kidd's automatic spoke at the same instant, but neither shot at the other. Wentworth's bullet smashed the microphone as the man shouted *"Ten!"* shouted the signal that was to send Nita to her death. He risked his life to save hers and he won. His bullet was a split second faster than the man's articulation. It smashed the microphone before the signal could be given!

The woman's bullet sped upward, blasting out the light. Wentworth flung himself backward out the door, tripped and fell. He rolled and within the room a machine gun racketed, thudding lead into the floor where he had fallen. The woman screamed commands. The bearded giant bellowed, and then the sounds were chopped off. The silence was more sudden than death.

Wentworth's eyes narrowed in the darkness as he sprang to his feet. His deduction had been partly right. He had figured that there must be a secret connection between these two buildings and the escape of these two, the sudden cessation of their shouts, proved him right. But he had been wrong in supposing that Nita was with the two leaders. Yet Nita was somewhere in these two buildings, he was sure. Somewhere? Yes, somewhere near the street where she could be thrust out to run the gauntlet of her executioners!

They would carry out their threat now, would kill Nita, for the Spider had failed in this attack! Despair heavy in his breast,

123

Wentworth sped down the stairs in a plunging run. He had sprung two traps in the first building and the woman had mentioned three. One of those traps had covered the roof entrance, the other had commanded the two entrances on the first floor. The third, he realized in a flash, must be in the basement. Probably the third would be baited with Nita herself—if they had not already sent her to her death!

As he raced again out the back door, vaulted the fence and crept, savagely intent, toward the first house again, his lips were drawn back from his teeth in a fierce snarl. This was the end of the battle, he swore to himself. He would find Nita and wipe out these leaders this time if the Spider died the next minute!

The violence of his oath checked Wentworth's red rage, fanned a cold, deliberate anger in its place. He proceeded more cautiously. He knew he must not only wipe out the leaders, but the gang also. Undoubtedly, they knew the methods of piracy that Captain Kidd's evil genius had devised. It would not be enough to destroy the leaders. No, his life was a sacrifice the Spider could not afford to make.

Even when he had rescued Nita, even if he succeeded in killing the leaders, he would be in the middle of a gang net that might well prove the end of the Spider. And the nation still would be endangered, its vital transportation crippled by the Pirates and their Green Fire out of hell. Thousands would still be slaughtered so their corpses could be stripped of wealth.

Besides those that perished, other thousands of innocents would suffer the pangs of grief, the bite of privation. Food supplies, vital commodities were being tied up and those, too, would cause want and stringency. The situation was ripe for revolution and already certain groups had seized the opportunity to work evil among the frightened and harassed people.

The fate of the nation might well hang on what the Spider accomplished in the next several minutes, whether he survived....

Into the darkness of the back hall, Wentworth crawled flat on his belly. He writhed to the basement door and inched it open. Below was blackness. Darkness had heralded each trap he had sprung so far. And the Spider must move cautiously if he were not only to spring this one harmlessly, but to steal the bait! God, to think that Nita was the bait! He eased through the door, on his feet now but moving in silence with his gun thrust before him.

SLOWLY HE descended until his feet found the end of the wooden steps and felt the damp cold of a concrete floor. Still there was no gleam of light, no sound to reveal the trap. He turned sharp to his right and stooped beneath the stairs. The steps were merely boards placed on the supports and had no backs. They would offer little protection, but Wentworth figured on them only to confuse gunfire. He drew a small flashlight from his kit, laid it on the steps, and clicked the button.

As if he had thrown the main switch of a gigantic battery of lights, his pressure flooded the basement with glaring brilliance! From a score of points the Pirates' dread chained lightning flashed its villainous Green Fire!

Wentworth crouched, gun tense in his hand, staring through the dazzle to learn from what point danger threatened. He made out figures vaguely through the blinding impact of the sudden light. On the point of firing, he caught himself up. One of those figures was a woman—it was Nita!

Even as he realized that fact, the guns scorched his palms, glittering with dancing Green Fire. He tried to cling to the weapons, but the heat was too great. He was forced to hurl his automatics to the floor! Trapped! He was trapped by the Green Fire he fought, caught in a basement and disarmed by electricity, by leaping inductive flames that made metal too hot for holding! On the point of victory, within sight of Nita, he was being worsted by a thing man's weapons could not fight!

He caught Nita's excited cry. "Quick, Dick! Get on wood! A platform, here!"

Already the Green Fire that spurted from every metallic thing in the room, that danced and glittered from pipes and wires and ran in little darting rivers across the floor, had stricken Wentworth's legs. His muscles knotted and writhed. Beneath his left arm, the tools of the Spider's kit began to burn his side.

With a despairing curse, Wentworth snatched at the leather packet, but before he hurled it frantically to the floor, he caught from it two tiny vials which he dropped into a pocket. His explosives! If they became superheated by those tools gleaming with the Green Fire, this house would tumble down about their ears.

He could see clearly now, could see Nita bound hand and foot and strapped to a chair that sat upon a long narrow wooden platform in the middle of the room. A man stood on either side of her with revolvers in their hands, revolvers that glittered with the Green Fire, but which they were able to hold because of bulky gloves.

"Oh, Dick, hurry!" Nita moaned. "Get to the platform!"

Get to the platform! Wentworth stared across twenty feet of concrete on which the Green Fire danced in hellish glee. The sputtering glare of the chained lightning intensified momentarily. The mounting stiffness of his body was almost overpowering. Any moment, Wentworth felt, his heart muscles would succumb to its slowly increasing potency. He managed to continue breathing only by violent effort.

He had walked into the trap, confident in his rage that he could tear apart any snare Captain Kidd had constructed. But he had not figured on this devilish ingenuity. He fought futilely to raise his arms, while the men on the platform jeered at him, mocking his struggles.

THE FATE of a nation, of countless thousands more who must die at the Pirates' hands if he fell, fought with Wentworth as he strained muscle-stiffened arms upward. If only he could reach those wooden steps, which would not conduct electricity. If he could reach them and drag his feet from contact with that dooming floor!

He would still be at the mercy of those glittering guns, but he would be free for a moment of the torturing grasp of the Green Fire. And each inch gained against an enemy was an inch nearer victory. At long last Wentworth's straining fingers clutched at the open wooden steps. He forced his hands to grip harder, flexed his pulsing arms and dragged himself clear of the fatal floor!

Instantly the shocking force of the Green Fire was broken, the kinks came out of his muscles. But the two men on the platform were laughing.

"You want to shoot him first, Hank?" one asked the other.

"Naw," said Hank. "Go ahead. After you, my dear Alphonse."

Wentworth set his lean jaw rigidly and began to swing his body in a wide arc, under the stairs and out, under and out. It was a slim chance he grasped at, a straw in a torrent that swept him and Nita and the nation's millions with them toward certain destruction!

"This is going to be fun," said the man who had spoken first. "I just love moving targets."

He raised his pistol deliberately and moved it with Wentworth's oscillations. Back under the stairs, the Spider's swing took him, then out into the open again. At the peak of his swing, he let himself go and flew, feet first, out over the electrically-charged floor! The man's gun spoke, but he had not anticipated the leap.

Wentworth struck the floor with one foot, bounded wildly and hit the edge of the platform. He stumbled and fell and the second shot blazed over his head.

He caught the gunman's legs and spilled him down upon himself as a shield, then hurled him bodily at his companion. The man could not dodge. The platform was too narrow. The two pirates spilled down in a shouting heap. Their feet touched the floor and they yelped with the pain of the shocks.

Wentworth was on his knees now. He flung savagely upon the two and now there was a grim smile on his face, the Spider's

128

fighting smile! A clawing hand tore the mask from his face, then his fist connected and the man called Hank was knocked cold! The other man fired point blank and Wentworth felt the hot shock of the lead burning his ribs. His fist hit the man's gun wrist, knocked the weapon from his hand. The Spider reached clenching fingers for the pirate's throat!

Two minutes later, he got slowly to his feet upon the platform, lips twisted in their hard, thin smile. He turned toward Nita and his eyes were burning. All about them played the ghastly Green Fire. The floor glittered with it and the shoes of the dead man, resting on the floor, began to smolder. Gently, but swiftly, Wentworth unfastened Nita's bonds. He snatched her tightly into his arms and for the moment fire and death and imminent disaster were forgotten in a kiss.

"You weren't hurt, dearest?" he asked.

The girl shook her chestnut curls slowly, blue eyes smiling.

"I wasn't even worried a whole lot," she said. "I knew you'd come."

Wentworth's smile left his face as he thought how nearly he had failed her. "We're not out of it," he said shortly. "They've got the whole city blockaded for a mile, gang cars with machine guns cruising the streets, shooting down every person they see moving. I don't know why police haven't got onto it yet."

Nita still smiled. "I haven't been here twenty minutes yet, Dick," she said. "It would take time to muster enough police to overcome a force of that size."

"Twenty minutes!" Wentworth stared, then smiled. "You're right. So much has happened, it seemed longer."

He stared down at the two men, dragged the feet of the one who was dead onto the platform to stop their smoldering. The scent was not pleasant. The very air seemed alive with electricity now. It was surcharged with ozone, and it made Wentworth feel queerly exhilarated, half drunken with a mad ecstasy of racing blood.

"We've got to get out of here and get out fast," he said curtly. "The super-supply of oxygen, generated by the electricity, will burn our lungs."

HE PICKED up his mask, and donned it and bent over the man he had knocked out. Already, due to the stimulation of the ozone, he was recovering from the heavy blow. Wentworth drew off the man's glove and found it made of heavy asbestos and rubber. He caught up one of the guns then and prodded the man called Hank. Hank's eyes opened dazedly. When he looked into the gun barrel, they reflected terrible fear.

Wentworth's masked face smiled slowly, and that smile was a fearful thing.

He slipped out his cigarette lighter and stooped over the man he had strangled, pressed its base to the yellowed forehead. When he removed the lighter, the red seal of the Spider gleamed wickedly.

"Either tell us how to turn off this electricity and help us to escape," Wentworth told his prisoner coldly, "or I'm going to put the seal on your forehead, too!"

The man began to tremble. "I don't know how," he said.

Wentworth yanked him to his feet.

"How would you like to step out into the Green Fire?" he asked softly.

"No!" It was a scream of fearful terror. "No, in God's name, Spider. Not that!"

Wentworth was still smiling.

"Please," Hank begged, "as heaven is my witness, *I don't know!*"

Wentworth stared fixedly into the man's terrified eyes and was forced to believe him. Good Lord, then they were still trapped! A machine gun wielded from those stairs could mow them down! By the flickering ghastly light, he searched the room feverishly.

His flashlight beam apparently had started this hell of Green Fire. This man knew of no switch. The only solution was that somewhere was hidden a photoelectric cell which was set to turn on the electricity at the first gleam of light. The flickering death dance of the Green Fire would keep the switch going. But if he could find it…. Abruptly he spotted a small black aperture in the wall directly opposite the stairs. He smashed a bullet through it. Darkness shut down upon the room!

Wentworth seized his prisoner and jabbed the gun against his ribs. Pushing him ahead, he escorted Nita to me steps. And suddenly he knew why there had come no interruption from above, no chattering machine gun from the steps, why no guns had spoken through hidden wall slits. Sirens wailed in the streets! The police had come!

He listened and heard the rattling volleys of pistols, the short savage bursts of machine guns. Now and then a bomb blasted with a rumbling concussion.

Wentworth kept a tight grip on the back of his prisoner's neck, his fingers gripped into the sockets beneath his ears. A quick squeeze there would in fifteen seconds cause such intolerable pain as to overpower a man.

WENTWORTH TOOK Nita and the prisoner into a dark room. They had only to wait a while now, wait until the battle was over and then send word to Kirkpatrick. True, there were men dead about here with the Spider seal upon their foreheads, but how could police say where the Spider was or what he looked like? He had worn a mask always before this gangster's eyes. Only when the man had been unconscious had he briefly been stripped of that mask.

As for Captain Kidd and her bearded partner, they probably would not escape the police battle. The man squirmed beneath his fingers and Wentworth tightened his hold, feeling the neck cords slide beneath his grip.

"Listen, Spider," the man quavered. "Let me go, will you? I'll make it worth your while."

Wentworth laughed. "You'll make it worth my while?" he gibed. "What are you going to offer the Spider?"

The man said, "Your life."

"What do you mean?" Wentworth's voice was quick and alert. His words sounded loud and he realized the constant rattle of gunfire had subsided. Wentworth felt a growing tension in his breast. Had he overlooked something? Was he to be snatched from the pinnacle in the very instant of victory?

The man sniggered.

"There was a movie camera in everyone of them traps," he

said. "It was set to start going when the lights went on and keep going until the lights was off. Captain Kidd said she wanted to keep a picture of you dying so she could enjoy her evenings at home."

"Well?" said Wentworth. "She didn't get a picture of me dying."

Then he recalled sharply what Captain Kidd had photographed. She had a motion picture of Richard Wentworth unmasked, killing a man and, afterwards, *printing the seal of the Spider on his forehead.*

His gasp and Nita's were simultaneous.

"Quick!" Wentworth snapped out. "Tell me where the camera was hidden and you can go free!"

In the silence that fell then between them, the silence and the darkness, he heard police orders shouted, heard men told to search all the houses. He gripped the man tightly.

"Okay," Hank whined. "Okay, I'll tell you!"

"Don't talk, Hank," a woman's voice bit into the room and Wentworth felt the man stiffen beneath his fingers. Instantly a gun leaped to the Spider's hand and he crouched, straining his eyes against the utter blackness.

"Don't forget the movie film, Spider," the woman spoke softly. "It would do you no good to kill me and then let those films come into police hands." The voice gained confidence. "You haven't time to force anyone to talk now, Spider, to tell you where the films are. Either you come to the door with your hands high and empty, or the police get those pictures!"

Wentworth's mind raced. That evidence would condemn him

133

beyond any doubt. It would doom Nita, too. Not only was she known as his fiancée, but she had been on the scene when he had killed, had embraced him there before the camera's eye and had seen him print the seal of the Spider upon the dead man's forehead!

So far as the killing itself was concerned, that could be justified in the eyes of the law. But there were scores of killings and other crimes, all committed to punish some criminal, to wreak the Spider's justice, which bore the Spider's seal. And those he would not be able to explain away.

"Hurry," came the woman's mocking voice from the doorway. "Will you surrender to our tender mercies? Or will you permit the police to see the film?"

WENTWORTH DID not hesitate. Better by far to brave the certainty of death at the hands of these gangsters, than to permit his identification as the Spider. For death would follow disgrace by police courts, too. Disgrace and death, and Captain Kidd would continue her piracy, her wholesale slaughter!

He was trapped, trapped in the moment of victory. When every point seemed won, when every obstacle seemed overcome, when police were taking charge of all about him, he was trapped. The criminals had been routed. The Pirates were in flight—and Wentworth and Nita—the Spider and his beloved—were prisoners of the fiends!

Wentworth spoke swiftly to Nita in an undertone. "It's death either way, darling, but one carries disgrace. If we choose to become the prisoners of the Pirates, I'm afraid there would be small chance of escape. They won't permit many chances to the Spider."

"Hurry." Captain Kidd was impatient. "The police will be here any minute now."

"For myself, Nita," Wentworth said, "there is no choice. I must continue the battle. If this woman has a way of escape—and she must have to wait so calmly—she can reorganize her forces and strike again. I must fight on, but you...."

Nita's hand closed on his in the dark. She pressed close to him and her arm slid across his shoulders. Her lips sought his.

"Where you go, Dick," she whispered against his mouth, "I go, too!"

Wentworth drew a quick breath. No use arguing to gain mercy for Nita. The woman would not permit anyone to remain behind to betray her.

"Three seconds," said the woman brusquely. "Three seconds and I go away and send the films to the police."

Wentworth was seeking frantically to find some way out. It was maddening to stand here in the dark talking calmly of a surrender that meant death and disgrace. He stalled for time, hoping against hope....

"You're losing confidence, Captain Kidd," he jeered. "Last time you gave me ten seconds!"

The woman said calmly, "Two seconds have elapsed. Quickly, what do you choose? To be my prisoners, or the prisoners of the State?"

Wentworth was trembling inwardly. Nita had left it for him to decide, had placed her life in his hands. *"Where you go, I go too.* "His hands clenched and the man, Hank, whimpered beneath the hard grip of his fingers.

"Time's up, Spider! What shall it be?" The woman he could not see was taunting him.

Wentworth cursed raggedly. He had had his moment of victory and it had slipped from his hands. He could not prevent this woman's Pirate crew from slaughtering and looting. He could do nothing. He was helpless. There could be but one answer. From the police there could be no escape this time. From the woman….

He hurled the prisoner from him violently, so viciously that the man sprawled upon the floor with a strangled cry. And then the Spider, raging, aflame with a fury that was the more intense because it was helpless, uttered two words he never before had pronounced, two words he never had expected to say even on the day of his death!

The Spider said, *"I surrender!"*

CHAPTER 15
PRISONER OF DISGRACE

THE WOMAN, still unseen in the darkness, laughed mockingly.

"I thought you'd decide it that way, Spider," she said. "And remember, no treachery. Three of my assistants know where the film is hidden and if anything happens to me, the film will go to the police."

Wentworth's lips were tight in a smile of self mockery. Those words had frozen in the bud another plan for escape. He had hoped to seize the woman, hold her as hostage for destruction of the film....

"Come to the door," the woman ordered, "and come with your hands high. Hank, get his gun and cover him from behind."

Wentworth's smile was bitter as he heard the man Hank say "Okay," heard his feet shuffle toward him through the darkness. A crook ordered, and the Spider obeyed slavishly, obeyed because he dared not do otherwise! It was inconceivable, but it was happening.

Death for himself, the Spider did not fear. He had prepared for it many times. He carried always those phials of explosive in his pockets and it had been his solemn pledge to himself that when the ultimate day came, when the Spider fell before his enemies, those explosives would destroy his body, wipe out any possibility that disgrace should strike his family, or his name, or those he loved.

Yes, he had prepared for death. But this time disgrace was certain, even if the explosives destroyed his body. But hope did not die. He would save his explosives. Swiftly he bent, snaking the phials from his pocket. He detached his garter from the sock and dragged it high on his thigh. Inside his thigh, where the elastic band gripped tightly, he thrust the phials.

"What are you doing?" Hank demanded suspiciously.

Wentworth took two long silent strides toward the door. "I'm over here," he said. "Hurry, will you, the police will be here any moment."

Nita's hand touched his arm and together they walked to the

door. Hank overtook them and got the Spider's gun. Instantly the white beam of a flashlight bathed them, held them for a full minute, then switched off.

"This way," the woman spoke sharply. "And remember trickery will mean the films will be turned over to the police!"

Wentworth felt his burning rage rise within him. But his anger, like his racing thoughts, was futile. For once his keen brain failed him. He must obey!

He followed the sound of Captain Kidd's sharp heels, Nita just behind him. Hank trailed in the rear. As they stole rapidly toward the rear of the house, police stumped into the forward doorway and lights swept up the stairs.

They ducked into the back yard—just in time. A policeman's hand torch sprayed light out through the doorway. By its reflected glow, Wentworth saw the woman ahead open a hidden gateway in the fence. She beckoned them into the house next door and down into its basement.

Wentworth's face was set now in self-mockery. Slowly, he calmed his wrath, forced himself to clear thought. He must accept the fact of his capture and seek a way out. He jerked his

Nita Van Sloan

shoulders in impatience as he ducked into a low passageway through the walls of the house itself and out beneath the street. A door closed and now a light was in the woman's hand.

Through the basement of another house, through a second tunnel they hurried and finally out into a street and a waiting auto. Wentworth felt sharp anxiety lest the police should stop them, he who had longed so for the law's interference! He had dodged police before, heaven knew, but never before had he wished for the escape of a criminal. Not until now had he tasted the ultimate gall of defeat!

Except to gesture Nita and Wentworth into the back of the car, to make sure that Hank got in, too, the woman paid them no attention. She drove herself. They came at last to an apartment house in the middle West Eighties, a five story affair with an automatic elevator that lifted them creakingly to the top floor.

The woman faced them for the first time in the light now, studied them with darkly amused eyes. She ducked a bow like a man's and waved a hand grandiloquently for their entrance into an apartment.

Wentworth made a queer figure as he returned the gesture, shirtless and with a disreputable coat upon his broad, square-set shoulders. Beneath that the precise formality of dress trousers with their thin line of satin striping down the outer seam was as mocking as was his docility in the presence of this crook. NITA ENTERED into the mockery of the occasion, elegant in her sweeping white gown beneath a gold and crimson opera cloak made from a mandarin's robe. She strolled into the apartment as into the halls of the Metropolitan Opera House.

Three men were on their feet as they entered. One was the bearded giant who towered six feet four even with his shaggy head thrust forward.

"What is this," he growled, "a party?"

The woman's voice was fraught with ugly laughter.

"It's a theater party, Bolo," she said, "a movie theater party. We came to admire the pictures the cameras took in the cellar. Let me introduce the Spider and his girl friend."

Bolo grated out a curse and advanced on Wentworth with the shambling movements of a great bear. The Spider turned a bored smile on Captain Kidd.

"Does he bite?" he asked. "Or is he just friendly that way?"

The woman laughed, admiration in her eyes. "Cut it, Bolo," she said. "You can't scare this baby."

Bolo stopped, undecided, and Wentworth turned away and found a chair for Nita, seated her gracefully.

"I think the show will start in a little while, dear," he said. "It comes right after this clown act, I believe." His back was an insult.

The two other men behind Bolo were grinning openly, but grinning so he could not see their faces. Both men were dapper and slight and obviously they were brothers.

"Our technicians," Captain Kidd introduced the two. "You must confess they did an able job on that cellar trap."

Wentworth raised his brows. He was completely master of himself now, eyes and brain alert. He smiled condescendingly. "It would have been better if they had concealed that pho-to-electric cell. A shot put it out of order and turned off the Green Fire."

The grudging admiration of the woman was reluctantly apparent on her face, but it was supplanted with anger, as if she feared to permit any kindlier feeling toward this suave man who, in their power, mocked them with their inferiority.

"We'll start the show," she said shortly. "There will be two acts." She turned to the man she had brought with them. "Come here, Hank," she said caressingly.

He cringed forward like an animal expecting the lash.

"Let me see the Spider's gun," she said softly.

The man handed it over, awkwardly, butt first. She took the weapon and, with it scarcely settled in her hand, fired point blank at the man. Hank screamed hoarsely and collapsed on the floor, gripping his thigh. The other three men blinked and their faces whitened slowly. It was apparent that even the giant Bolo was frightened.

Nita turned her head, and Wentworth's grim lips set rigidly. He had seen this woman in action before. But he had never before seen such an expression as gleamed in her eyes now. It was a gloating madness and he realized abruptly that the woman must be a psychopathic case. She would delight in the suffering of others. She was a sadist of the worst type!

Her snake-like lips writhed as she smiled down on the whimpering victim of her torture-lust. "I just broke your femur, Hank," said Captain Kidd softly. "You are to be the first act of our little show, and I didn't want you to get restless. Bolo, shove that table over here."

THE BEARDED giant caught a heavy table with one hand and whirled it into the middle of the floor.

"Now put our friend Hank on it," she said, "and tie him there."

Hank was half-fainting from the wound in his leg. Blood spread a widening stain on his trousers.

"I ain't done nothin'," he begged. "I ain't done a thing. I didn't get the Spider, but I fixed it so you could."

The woman said nothing and Bolo scooped him up from the floor, his broken leg dangling horribly, and slapped him down on the table. Hank fainted and ropes were thrown tightly over his body while he was out, Wentworth looked on with hard, ugly glints in his gray-blue eyes. He knew this was a foretaste of what faced them, and he thought grimly of the explosive strapped against his thigh.

"Bring him out of it," the woman said impatiently. "He's got to know what's happening and why."

Water sloshed into the man's face and he rolled his head and opened his eyes feebly.

"Hank," said Captain Kidd slowly, "you are going to die with the flag on your chest."

Hank gazed up into the mask-like white of his chiefs face and moaned.

"The flag, Hank, and you know the reason." She paused, but the man made no sound but his whimpering moan. "You were going to sell us out to save your own worthless hide. You offered to show the Spider where the films were hidden. It would have done no good because the films were already gone. But in intent you were a traitor. So the flag!"

The flag. Wentworth knew what that meant, remembered the skull and crossbones carved with a burning knife blade on a boy's young flesh and a girts white breasts!

As she spoke, the woman stooped and snatched her skirt to her knee, snaked a gleaming knife from her garter. She poised it over Hank's chest.

"Gag him," she ordered.

Her breasts were panting now with horrible emotion, straining against the venomous yellow silk with which she habitually clothed herself. Her eyes were heavy lidded and as a gag was bound cruelly into Hank's mouth the tip of a pale tongue slid out and touched the blood red of her lips.

Wentworth felt the blood pounding hard and slowly in his head, felt the throb of that old scar across his temple and knew its thin white tracery was an angry red. He fought a battle within himself. The man was a criminal, had tried to kill the Spider, yet....

"Listen," he said crisply, "that man only did what any other man would have done. He wanted to save his life, and he offered what he had to buy me off."

The woman turned her head slowly as a snake's. "Keep your mouth shut," she said in an even, flat voice, "or I'll carve a flag on your girl friend's breasts!"

Wentworth heard Nita's breath suck in, felt the tightening bulge of his own shoulder muscles. He gazed straight into the woman's eyes, scarcely visible beneath drooping lids, and felt the chill of her madness, of her bloodlust trace out his spine with cold fingers. He met her stare equally and presently the moaning of the woman's victim pulled her gloating gaze back to the man on the table.

With a single swift movement, she ripped open Hank's shirt, moved the dagger slowly closer to the chest. As it neared his flesh, the blade began to glow greenly and little livid sparks played along the blade. The man on the table tossed his head, whimpering animal sounds through the gag. The blade touched his body, and the singeing, burning odor of scorched human flesh rose nauseatingly into the room!

THE TWO technicians sat white-faced, eyes fascinated upon the torture of their fellow workman. Bolo stood with panting chest, staring down at the design the woman's slow blade traced upon the living flesh of her victim. With the abruptness of a shot, that chest ceased to move. The tossing head, the clenching fingers were still, and the man's entire body went lax within the bonds.

The woman ripped out a curse as searing as her knife and plunged the blade violently into the man, once, twice, and again. She straightened slowly then, and wiped the blade upon the dead man's torn clothing. She stood for a moment, staring heavy-lidded at Wentworth and at Nita, her breasts panting with slow, deep breaths.

Words squeezed from between her red, restless lips.

"No," she seemed to be giving orders to herself. "No, not yet, not yet! There are other uses for him." Her eyes clung to Nita.

Wentworth turned carelessly from the woman to the men. "Got a cigarette, Bolo?" he asked casually. "This is the intermission, I believe."

His words seemed to jerk the people in the room from their trance of horror. Bolo stared at him, then laughter rumbled deep in his throat.

"I've got some chewing tobacco," he said heavily. "Want a plug?"

Wentworth smiled slightly. "I gave that up when I began to travel in society. I'm afraid I'll have to forego the pleasure." He turned to the woman who was leaning now, a little weakly, against the table on which lay the body of her recent victim.

"When do we see the second act?" he asked. "I hope it's more interesting than the first."

The woman permitted herself to smile. She straightened away from the table and slowly slid the knife into its sheath against a graceful leg.

"It should be more interesting," she said slowly. "It will depict yourself, dear Spider, killing a man and printing that childish little red seal of yours upon his forehead!"

CHAPTER 16
THE SECOND ACT

WENTWORTH KNEW the woman was toying with him, taunting himself and Nita before the kill, secure in her knowledge that he would not strike so long as the film was in her hands. She was indulging in the sadism that had moved her so horribly in her torture of the underling who had attempted to betray her.

But nothing of this showed on his clean-lined intelligent face. It was as perfect a mask as ever, not the rigid, expressionless poker face that betrays itself by its very stiffness. Wentworth masked his feelings in mobility, by curving his features into the portrayal of other emotions than those which might tear at his vitals. His face showed polite interest. Within him, despair such as the Spider had never before known grew and expanded until it shook his whole being, despair for himself and for Nita.

He drew a chair nonchalantly beside Nita and leaned back as if prepared to enjoy a show. The woman made hurried preparations, wheeled a small projection machine from a closet and focused it on the opposite wall. She reached into the closet then and took out a film box. Wentworth got to his feet, and the woman glared at him. But he only walked over to the body upon the table, patted the man's side pockets and found a bulge.

He smiled at the woman.

"Cigarettes," he explained.

He took them from the dead man's pocket, strolled back to Nita. The woman saw him seated. She did not see him draw his cigarette lighter. While apparently lighting the cigarette, with his eyes focused on its end, he watched her as she prepared the film. She unwound a strip of it and fastened it to a second spindle. Then Wentworth sprang!

His movement was swift and soundless as a cat and he held the blazing lighter before him. The woman whirled. But Wentworth had already set his lighter down beneath the spindle with its load of celluloid film. He seized the woman in his arms and wrestled her away. Behind him the flame blazed up, hot and yellow. The film that held the Spider captive was afire!

The woman writhed and twisted in his grip, striking viciously with her high heels. Wentworth snatched up her skirt and snaked the knife from her garter. He found a button on its end and pressed it with his thumb, turned its point toward the woman's heart.

Bolo was half across the room toward him; the two brothers were starting to their feet.

"Stay where you are!" Wentworth snapped. "Or I'll carve a Spider on Captain Kidd's heart!"

Green Fire was sputtering along the knife blade. The woman he held prisoner ceased to fight and stood rigid within his imprisoning left arm.

"Is the film burned entirely, Nita?" Wentworth asked casually.

Nita got up calmly from her chair and walked past Wentworth toward where the film still sent flickering light playing over the ceiling.

"Yes," she said, "but I'm afraid your lighter is done for. It's quite fused."

Wentworth shook his head, frowning. "I'm sorry about that lighter," he said. "Captain Kidd, I'll have to trouble you to come with me."

He started to back across the room. The woman moved without resistance.

"Bolo," said the woman casually, "will you send those other two rolls of film to Kirkpatrick? I think he would be interested."

Wentworth continued his slow backing across the room, until he reached the door. "If you send those films, your leader dies," he told Bolo shortly.

THE GIANT was following him step by step, white teeth gleaming through his tangled black beard. In the corner of his eye, Wentworth saw Nita, realized suddenly that she would be blocked from the door until he had passed because of the smoldering fire about the projection machine. He checked, started forward—too late!

Bolo sprang forward and flung his brawny arms about Nita and he, too, seized a knife from his belt and pointed it toward Nita's heart, pointed a blade that began to glimmer with Green Fire!

"Take your choice," said Captain Kidd calmly, twisting her head so that Wentworth could see the corner of her sneering red mouth. "Stab me and Nita dies and the film goes to Kirkpatrick. Release me and Nita may go free. Nita may, but you must remain."

Wentworth stood rigid, clasping the woman immovably against his chest, the knife glittering a ghastly Green Fire over his face as its set, grim lines showed above her shoulder. Facing him, the bearded giant held Nita in an exactly identical pose, the knife so close that the front of Nita's dress began to brown slightly from the scorching heat of the blade. If she felt any pain, she gave no indication. Her eyes met Wentworth's bravely, her lips smiling slightly.

"Go ahead, Dick," she said. "Take that woman out. I don't believe they have another film and with her in your power, the gang will be broken."

Ah, but she was brave! A fitting mate for the Spider. Coolly, she told him to go, though she knew that his departure meant her own death. Wentworth felt his heart surge within him at the sight of her brave, smiling face, her eyes unafraid upon his own.

As he watched, the knife thrust even closer to Nita's breast and despite her bravery, her tips twitched at the searing heat. Sweat started on Wentworth's brow. He dug his own knife closer against the woman's chest and smelled the singeing cloth.

"Don't, Bolo, you fool!" the woman spat out. "If you burn the girl, he's going to burn me, too!"

Wentworth said quietly, "You get the idea perfectly."

When Bolo eased the blade an inch away, he did the same. His jaws were locked in anguish. Many times before he had been forced to decide between his love for Nita and his service to humanity. Many times, but the fierce pain of that choice never lessened, never abated.

Should he force the issue, drag this woman from the room and leave Nita captive in the hands of these mad killers? Should he go and risk the sending of the film to Kirkpatrick? Coldly, sweat starting to his brow, he weighed the issue of his own disgrace and Nita's death against the victory of capturing and slaying this woman. Nita knew what wavered in the balance and once more she smiled bravely.

"Go ahead, Dick," she said.

But Wentworth doubted that killing this woman would wreck the gang. Evidently these men knew the operation of the Green Fire as well as she did. Her hold over them was obviously terror, and this man Bolo might well carry on in her place.

A terrible indecision racked Wentworth. Never before had there been a wavering in his path, never hesitation in the sure, swift execution of his duty. But to see Nita die in horrible torture before his eyes!

Wentworth grinned savagely. Wild laughter poured from his lips, then ceased. He forced words between his locked teeth.

"Release Nita, and I will remain," he said. "Take her to the door and permit her to leave."

"You swear that," demanded Captain Kidd swiftly.

"No, Dick, no!" Nita cried. "Can't you see she's bluffing? She hasn't got the film! Take her and go! Leave me here!"

Wentworth's tortured eyes met Nita's across the shoulder of the woman he held prisoner. Nita's lips trembled in a smile.

"Don't forget our promise to each other, Dick!" she urged. "I am nothing. When death threatens me, you are to forget I mean anything to you. Let me die!"

CAPTAIN KIDD uttered a sneering laugh, but it did not ring true. Despite herself, she admired the courage of this lovely girl who did not fear death.

Wentworth's eyes clung to Nita's. Never had Nita seemed so lovely, standing superbly erect there with that knife against her bosom, her proud head thrown back, her blue eyes tender upon his. And slowly Wentworth smiled, a smile ineffably gentle.

"No, darling," he said, "it is not necessary. I have a plan. Go, dear, and don't worry further about me. Hurry, Nita, hurry! Go!"

There was a sudden fierce urging in Wentworth's voice. Nita gazed intently into his eyes, gazed and was convinced by the confidence he put upon his face, was deceived by the cheerful smile which he, the master of facial masks, painted upon his lips.

She nodded slowly. "Whatever you say, Dick."

"Swear it, Spider!" the woman demanded sharply.

"I swear," he said precisely.

And because the Spider always kept his word, because crook-dom which distrusted even its own brother, which hated the Spider as it did death itself, and feared him as it did not fear death, because these criminals knew that the Spider's word, once plighted, always was fulfilled, Bolo's arm and knife dropped; and Nita, unhampered, walked slowly past Wentworth to the door. With her hand on the knob, she paused a moment, gazing back at Wentworth.

"Go," he said hoarsely.

Nita nodded, smiled confidently, and went out the door.

Wentworth let the breath whistle between his teeth. He thrust the woman roughly from him, hurled her half across the room and dropped the knife to his side. The woman whirled and stared at him with her red lips drawn back viciously from her teeth.

"Kill him, Bolo!" she snarled. "I'll take care of the girl!" She darted toward the door.

Wentworth's leap was faster. He reached the door and flung the woman across the room with a jerk that slammed her against the wall. Her eyes rolled up and she slumped, almost fell. He dropped the blade of the knife, no longer glittering with the Green Fire since he had released the button in its hilt. As the men darted toward him, he ripped the inner side of his left trouser leg, snatched out the two vials and raised them above his head in a clenched fist. The Spider laughed wildly, madly.

"Come on!" he cried as the men halted in their charge, staring wild eyed at the little bottles he clenched in his hand.

"Come on," Wentworth taunted again. "These bottles contain only trinitrotoluene, which is ten times more powerful than T.N.T.!"

From the mad glare of his eyes, the three men shrank back. Even the woman, recovering from his blow, cringed from the threat of those two tiny bottles.

"Stand there," said Wentworth violently. "Or, as God is my witness, I'll blow us all to hell!"

He laughed wildly again.

"The Spider swears it!"

CHAPTER 17
THE SPIDER'S COFFIN

T HE THREE men and the woman stood cringing with frozen terror, staring wide-eyed at this madman who was willing to destroy himself if only his enemies died with him. The Spider had sworn it.

"You wouldn't do it," the woman said hoarsely, but there was hopelessness in her voice.

Wentworth laughed sharply. "Why do you suppose I got Nita out of the room?" he demanded. "I do not fear death myself. And this death would not disgrace the Spider. There would be nothing left of his to identify the Spider as Richard Wentworth."

"If we give you the films," said Bolo hoarsely, "will you go away and leave us?"

Wentworth smiled slowly and shook his head.

"No, Bolo," he said, "you four are going with me to the street and we are going together to police headquarters."

The woman was crouched like a cat against the wall, her lips writhing. "If we go, the films go to Kirkpatrick," she said fiercely.

Wentworth's smile did not fade. "Then, the best thing to do would be to destroy us all right here."

Captain Kidd laughed suddenly. The sound of it strengthened her. She straightened away from the wall and walked boldly toward Wentworth.

"Give me that explosive, Spider," she said. "Here is something you did not think of. The films are not here. If we die, they go to Kirkpatrick and they will disgrace you even though you are dead. *They will send Nita to the electric chair!*"

Wentworth's eyes narrowed, and the woman came on. "The other films aren't here, Spider. They are in the hands of other members of the gang… And they have their orders."

The door knob behind Wentworth creaked tinnily and he sprang away from it. The woman sprang at the same instant, grabbing at the hand that held the explosives. A man charged heavily from the rear and seized the wrist, too. Wentworth lashed out behind him with the knife, felt it gouge into living flesh. Then lights exploded before his eyes as a terrific blow caught him on the head. Darkness came after the light, soft, impenetrably black darkness that swept up over his brain like bottomless waters….

WORDS FROM incalculable distance beat in slowly upon his dim consciousness like feeble waves. That was his next memory after the blow. He fumblingly tried to understand the words, tried to remember. Then his senses rushed upon him. Warily he kept his eyes shut, and strained to understand those words.

"We got to get away from here in a hurry," the woman said. "We'll leave Donaghue's body and the Spider here. This lighter of his will still work and we'll put the seal on Donaghue's forehead and shoot the Spider with Donny's gun. That will take care of both of them."

Donaghue! Was it possible that Captain Kidd meant the

same fat detective who time and again had crossed his path in his battle with the Pirates? He listened curiously.

"Sure, I know he threw in with us," the woman was saying impatiently, "sold out to us when his agency stumbled across some dope we wanted. And he put the flag on that little witch, Nellie, for us...."

A man cursed querulously. "Hell, I can't thank him for that. I had my eye on her. She had everything, that dame. Brains, too. You said she was the one saw the money in old Curley's transformer, and even pointed out how we could work the trick by pretending to kidnap her...."

"You through?" Captain Kidd asked softly.

The man gulped, spluttered excuses. Through the ache and dazzle of the pain in his head, Wentworth began to fill out the picture. He knew that girl, Nellie, who had been killed hadn't had the intelligence to figure out such a scheme. She had fallen into the hands of this woman in some way, probably through her gangster friend, Dutch Brogard. Captain Kidd, for some reason, had seen fit to give the girl the credit for the fake kidnapping....

The woman spoke with slow venom. Her voice dripped hate.

"Nellie did a good job, sure," she said, "but she was dangerous. The police were after her with a good description. We found that out from a stoolie we got on the force. Then this Spider was around the neighborhood of old Curley's home asking questions. Right after that, police started watching around there, and looking for Nellie and Dutch Brogard. Both of them had to be rubbed out for our own safety. If the police had traced us through them, as the Spider did tonight, all the money we've taken wouldn't do us any good at all."

It wasn't like this woman to make explanations. Wentworth wondered why she went to such lengths to justify a thing that really needed no explanation. If the two were dangerous to them, it was good gangster tactics to get rid of them. He heard his own name....

"That Spider must have eyes in the back of his head," the querulous one was saying.

"Yeah, he sure must," growled the basso of Bolo. "He stabbed Donaghue right through the heart."

"Everybody satisfied now?" Captain Kidd asked sarcastically, and Wentworth knew the white terror of her underlings that would meet her impatience. When that woman spoke, none dared oppose her.

"All right," she snapped. "Terry, get in the coffin!"

Wentworth almost opened his eyes at that order. Putting a live man in a coffin!

"You got your orders straight now?" the woman asked.

A man's thin voice said, "Sure. I stay in the coffin until I hear the Green Fire crackle three times. Then I hop out and stop the train."

Wentworth started with a twitch of muscles that was almost physical. He knew now how they stopped the trains, knew that tonight, with the Spider finally disposed of, the Pirates planned to kill and rob again! But he did not know where the blow would fall, what train they would attack....

"That's right," said Captain Kidd. "Climb in the coffin now

and we'll ship you away from here. That girl of the Spider's is apt to be coming back before long. She won't bring the police for fear of the films, but she'll have some friends to help. Let's be clear by then."

There was the sound of scrambling feet, then wood hitting wood.

"Okay," said the woman. Wentworth heard her steps coming toward him, felt her fingers dig at his eyes. They hurt like hell, but he gave no sign of life.

"He'll stay like that a while. Come on," she said. "We'll get those guys to carry the coffin. Henry, stay here."

NOT UNTIL Wentworth heard feet clump across the room did he cautiously open his eyes. A man, evidently the one she called Henry, was examining the tubes of the Spider's explosive with careful hands. He held them up to the light and his back was half turned toward Wentworth. His gun lay on the table a half dozen feet away.

Wentworth surged to his feet and reeled, blinded by the pain his sudden movement stabbed through his battered head. He overcame that with gritted teeth, without the loss of a second sprang toward the man he only half saw and seized the explosives with both hands.

The man turned wild eyes toward him, let go the explosives and sprang sideways toward the table and his gun. He got the gun while Wentworth was leaping toward him again. The gun flashed up, but Wentworth's movement was swifter. While he plunged the explosives into his pocket with his right hand, he struck at the revolver with his other. The bullet ploughed the floor between their feet.

Wentworth brought both hands to bear on the revolver then, seized gun and wrist and twisted. The gun leaped and blasted in their joint grasp, then the pirate let go and reeled backward, hands clasped to his belly. The Spider stood panting, pistol swinging in his left hand while the man collapsed—and heard wood grate behind him!

He twisted his body, and looked into the muzzle of an automatic, gripped by a man who sat in the coffin. Wentworth knew then what the sound had been. He had heard the raising of the coffin lid! Even as that thought flashed through his mind, he jerked up the gun awkwardly behind him and fired.

The mouth of the man who sat in the coffin flew open in a choking gasp. His eyes bulged wide with surprise, then rolled up as if he sought to see that blue hole that gaped in his forehead where Wentworth's bullet had pierced. Then he slumped over the edge of the coffin and slow drops of blood squeezed out and splashed on the carpet.

Wentworth stood reeling on his feet, the hand that clasped the revolver pressed to his aching forehead. The walls were thick, but those shots might be heard, might bring the pirates back. They probably had gone to the first floor of the apartment house for men to carry the coffin, but it would not take them long to ascend in the swift automatic elevators.

Blearily, he stared at the bodies of the two men he had killed, at the body of Donaghue on the floor, and a slow smile twisted Wentworth's lips, a grim and menacing smile. He stripped off his clothing and that of the man in the coffin. He put his own clothing on the body, made a small mixture of the explosive in one of the bottles and laid it on the man's chest close against his chin. He yanked up the body of the first man he had killed and staggered to the window, tossed it to a roof two stories below.

Then he climbed into the coffin, pulled the lid almost down and through the opening fired a bullet into the tiny tube of explosive on the chest of the corpse. The jar of the explosion knocked the coffin off the chairs on which it rested. Wentworth heard the door flung open in the same instant and swiftly felt over the fastenings of the coffin lid. He found that he could control them absolutely from inside. He locked them and closed his eyes to ease the pounding ache of his head. Little flashes of light danced in his brain. Not until that moment did he consider the fact that he had crawled into a coffin! Even now that he began to think of it, there was no shudder of horror. For the Spider, that coffin was a haven of refuge!

FEET POUNDED across the floor, and he heard Captain Kidd grating curses.

"That damned Spider has got blown up with his own stuff," she ground out. "But where's Henry?"

"The window's open," came Bolo's gruff rejoinder.

Feet pounded to the window and the curses ripped out again. Wentworth lifted his voice inside the coffin in muffled imitation of Terry's tones.

"What happened?" he demanded querulously. "The locks of this damned lid got jammed when that explosive let go."

"What's the matter?" the woman demanded close against the lid.

"The locks are jammed. I can't open the damned thing," Wentworth complained.

"Do you think you can if you work on them awhile?" she asked.

"I guess so," said Wentworth, still imitating Terry's thin querulous voice. "What happened?"

"The Spider got blown up with his own explosive," said Captain Kidd. "We can't hang around now. Radio cars will be on our necks in two jumps. We'll hurry you out of here."

Wentworth felt the coffin heaved up and carried rockingly across the floor. A tight smile twisted his mouth. The Spider was escaping from one of the tightest jams in a life of peril. And, in doing it, he was being carried to the scene of the Pirates' next raid! He relaxed and rested while the coffin jogged along. Finally it was set down.

"You got the films?" He heard Bolo's heavy voice.

"Yes," the woman replied. "You carry one set and I'll carry the other. When we get through tonight, we'll send them to Kirkpatrick. We ought to take nearly a million tonight. We'll let that pilot train with soldiers drift by and burn them out at the same time we take the train itself."

Wentworth quivered as those words reached his ears. They had not bluffed about the films then! Even if he thwarted their attack on the train, he must then run down these two leaders and wrest the films from them or he and Nita would be doomed!

He cursed under his breath as he felt the coffin lifted again, heard it slide along a floor that vibrated, heard the hum of a motor.

The woman spoke close to the coffin top. "You got those locks fixed?"

Wentworth cursed shrilly. "It'll take another hour," he said. "That explosion jammed them."

"Okay," said the voice. "You'll be on the train in half an hour and you'll have an hour after that before we turn on the juice. Rest in peace," she finished mockingly, and then the coffin jounced and Wentworth knew the truck, or hearse, was moving.

The Spider, sealed in a coffin, was on his way to triumph—or to death!

CHAPTER 18
THE COFFIN OPENS

WITHIN A half hour, as the woman had promised, he was on the train, and with a jolt and a creak, the train got under way.

It was close and hot inside the coffin, but air seeped in through a hidden ventilation slit so that Wentworth had no serious trouble in breathing. After minutes that seemed to stretch into interminable days, he heard the hollow roar of the train in a tunnel give way to the rocking jar of smooth tracks. They were racing out into the open country now, he knew. How long before the Pirates would strike? An hour after the train had started, she said. Great God! Did he have to stay in this coffin another three quarters of an hour?

The close confinement of the tight box that held him, the inability to move hand or foot more than a few inches, was maddening. He could breathe, but the hot closeness of the scanty air was a torture to his lungs, to his aching head. All his iron-willed control was necessary to resist the jangled nerves which cried out to throw the lid of the coffin wide and spring from this close prison.

Wentworth fought that feeling for minutes that were hours long. The time was not yet ripe, he told himself over and over. If he sprang from this box of the dead too soon, he would be seized, probably accused of being one of the Pirates. His chances of saving the train would be lost—of catching the criminals and ending that dread reign once and for all would be ruined!

After an eternity of waiting, he heard men moving about and presently the reedy voice of a boy.

"Okay," the voice said, "if Apollo's got to stay here, I'm staying too!"

Wentworth felt a thrill of hope race through him. He knew that thin voice. It was Jim Walsh! If he had Apollo with him, it meant that Nita must be near, too. He would have help then in his battle with the Pirates! He strained his ears, heard the men laughingly assent.

"But keep that muzzle on the dog," one of them warned. "He's certainly an ugly looking brute!"

How much, Wentworth wondered, did Nita know or guess? Undoubtedly, she had trailed the coffin to this train. But she could not be aware that he was in it. If she knew what had happened in that room of horror in the apartment, she must think him dead. She must think that he had taken the last resort and blown himself up!

How many minutes had passed since the train got under way? He began to calculate swiftly. From fifteen to twenty minutes would be needed to get through the tunnels and maze of the yards and since that time, Jim had found his way to the baggage car and made friends with the men on guard here. Great heavens! Had he, fighting the frantic cry of his body for release from the close confines of the coffin, been too Spartan in his stoicism? Had he stayed in the coffin too long? The train must have been under way for almost forty minutes of that allotted hour!

If he were to save the people of this train from the Green Fire, from the singeing horror of that fearful chained lightning, he must act quickly! Tight in his coffin, evidently lined with asbestos and rubber against the fury of that super-voltage, high amperage current of the Green Fire, he would be safe.

But it was not for that he had risked disgrace and death a thousand times over. He must save these innocents speeding aboard this train, save Nita and Jim, and capture the Pirates. He had a plan, but he would be working against terrific odds. He must hurry, hurry!

HE UNFASTENED the locks of the coffin lid and pressed it upward a fraction of an inch, peered out into the dimly lighted baggage car.

He saw that Jim was walking around idly, talking to the dog and gradually making his way toward the coffin. What the boy expected to find there, Wentworth had no idea. Perhaps he carried a gun that he was to fire into the box....

When Jim was quite near, Wentworth called his name softly.

"Jim," he said, "don't make a sound. It's the Spider!"

The boy stiffened. His mouth fell open. Once more Wentworth warned him to remain quiet, talking in a swift undertone that the rhythmic clacking of the wheels covered.

"Come here, Jim," said Wentworth.

Trembling, white of face, frightened, the boy advanced rigidly toward the coffin.

"Geez, Spider, is it really you?" he asked quaveringly. "Are you alive?"

"Of course," said Wentworth impatiently, but even as he spoke he felt a grim amusement at the boy's timid words. Then Nita and Jim had believed the Spider dead! And fearlessly, Nita was carrying on his work! Wentworth felt a thrill of pride in her, in this brave boy.

Jim came quite close and Wentworth whispered again.

"Are Miss Nita and Ram Singh on the train?" he asked.

The boy nodded, jerked a glance over his shoulder at the baggage men. But they were busy, shifting luggage and trunks. The dog Apollo sat on his haunches where he was tied by the far wall, watching Jim with steadfast eyes.

"Miss Nita is," said Jim rapidly, "but Ram Singh isn't."

Wentworth thought swiftly for a moment, then made up his mind.

"Tell Miss Nita to come here. Tell her about me and that

the Pirates are going to strike any minute, so that she must move fast. Tell her to come here!"

Jim ducked his head in a swift nod, his eyes going wide at the mention of the Pirates. Then he turned and walked very carelessly over to Apollo, strolled out of the baggage car. The men called after him jokingly and he jeered back and was gone.

Swiftly, Wentworth fashioned a mask out of a handkerchief, held his revolver ready and slammed back the coffin lid with a clatter! He sat bolt upright and leveled the revolver.

The two men whirled, hands snatching for their guns.

"Put them up, high," Wentworth snapped.

There was a stunned paralysis on the men's faces. The leveled revolver, the man speaking from the coffin stultified their senses! Slowly, as Wentworth repeated the order, their hands went up. Deliberately, cautiously, he clambered from the coffin and moved toward them. He lined the pair up facing the side wall of the car, swiftly took their weapons.

Apollo recognized him and strained eagerly at his leash, but he was quiet as Wentworth had trained him to be. He took the dog's leather thong without for a moment relaxing his guard upon the two men. One-handed, he rigged a noose in each end of the leash and made the trainmen cross their hands behind them. A quick throw of the noose, a jerk, and they were helpless. He bound them swiftly, and when Jim brought Nita he was in complete charge of the situation.

She came to him swiftly, her eyes bright, every movement of her shapely body eager. Wentworth sprang to meet her, clasped her close in his arms and, for a moment, he removed his handkerchief mask.

"Say, what is this?" demanded one of the baggage men from where he lay helpless on the floor. "A holdup or a petting party?"

Wentworth laughed happily at that challenge. But it was only for a second. Seconds were precious now. Every moment they were racing nearer and nearer to the trap of the Pirates, every moment the clicking wheels rolled nearer to the contacts that would send the Green Fire leaping through every inch of this train, killing, burning, paving the way for the looting of the dead!

He kept Jim in the shadows. The trainmen had not seen Nita's face. Wentworth's body had interposed, and he made Nita cover her lovely features with a handkerchief mask also, told her swiftly of his plans. The train must be emptied of every living soul except himself. He would use the coffin for protection, run the train into the Pirate trap, and then—the Spider's vengeance!

"But, Dick, how...."

"Shush," Wentworth told her quickly, "there's no time. You stay here until I call you. Don't let the engineer come back into the train." He gave her a gun.

"Listen," called one of the baggage men, "are you Pirates or what are you?"

Wentworth halted in his swift stride toward the exit door of the baggage coach, stared at the men. If he could convince them of his good faith, they might help. And he faced a tremendous undertaking, emptying the train single-handed. The instant the train stopped, the pilot coaches full of soldiers running ahead smoothly now would come shooting back, men armed with machine guns and rifles would pile to the right of way and swoop down upon him.

Yet he dared not speed on along the tracks much farther for fear that the Pirates would turn on their deadly Green Fire! He jerked his head. No, there was no time to make sure of these men. He must work alone.

"I'm fighting the Pirates," he said swiftly, "but any moment now they may strike. There's no time to argue."

He raced on toward the door, stripped off his mask. He had no time to disguise himself, nothing to work with now that his kit was gone. Yet he could not walk through the aisles with a white handkerchief tied over his face. His costume would draw stares, too. A pair of bloodstained trousers, a greasy coat drawn over a silken undershirt, patent leather shoes. But there was no time, no time!

He yanked off the handkerchief, turned up his collar and strode swiftly through the day coaches in the forward part of the train. People were sprawled on the seats. They stared at him curiously as he strode by, seeking the conductor. He stopped a porter, asked directions. The man stared at him and then slowly grinned. He bowed, touching his forehead with a cupped palm.

"*Salaam, sahib,* the Spider," he said impassively.

CHAPTER 19
"THE PIRATES ARE COMING!"

WENTWORTH GRABBED the porter's shoulders with a joy such as had not been his in days.

"Ram Singh!" he cried.

He was overjoyed to have the redoubtable Hindu at his side in this perilous adventure. But there was no time to ask or give explanations. Somehow the Hindu had followed the trail Wentworth had planted for him and in the crisis he was on hand. He had overpowered or bribed a porter and taken his place.

Quickly, Wentworth outlined the danger that threatened, the mounting threat of each moment's delay. Horrible death was racing toward them, racing with the speed of the chained lightning that could strike so terribly.

"The conductor's two cars back," Ram Singh said swiftly and together they moved through the swaying aisles, ignoring the stares that met them. They found the conductor, a grave-faced gaunt man with coal black hair. Some suspicion must have flashed through his mind as the two strode toward him, for he reared up, hand going beneath his coat.

Ram Singh leaped forward, jabbed a gun against his belly and Wentworth strode to him.

"Listen," he said, "I have no time to argue. The Pirates are going to strike any minute. They electrocute everyone on the trains. I'm fighting them and you must help."

The man opened his mouth and began a frightened protest. Wentworth growled a curse. There was no time for this! Minutes, seconds brought fearful death nearer. This man could help them if he would not argue. Wentworth tried swiftly to convince the man, but he was suspicious. He only glared and argued.

"Into the smoker," snapped Wentworth.

Ram Singh jostled the man backward down the narrow hallway, into the empty smoker. As they thrust into the room, the conductor, swearing, made a frantic wrench for his gun. Ram Singh hit him heavily on the head and the gaunt official crumpled.

Swiftly then, Wentworth stripped him of his uniform and while he got into it, Ram Singh bound and thrust the conductor into the toilet, locked the door shut upon him. If the Green Fire struck too soon, he was doomed. But so were they all! Wentworth and Ram Singh and Nita and Jim and four hundred others who braved the steel trails that had become more perilous even than the Spanish Main in days of old.

Wentworth darted from the smoker and yanked on the air signal cord to the engineer, ordering slow speed. That was better than stopping at once. It might cause questions ahead in the cabin of the locomotive, might cause the soldiers ahead to become suspicious, but as long as the train moved, neither engineer nor soldiers would interfere. And it kept the Green Death more seconds away.

"You go forward, Ram Singh," Wentworth said swiftly. "Tell everyone that we've discovered the Pirates are going to strike and that every soul must get off. Get them bunched together in the aisles and when I stop the train, push them off fast.

"If you run into any government men—I know there are

some on board—you'll have to take care of them as if they were recalcitrant passengers. A quick blow with the blackjack and dump them out with the others. Make passengers carry them. Then get forward and chase the engineer and fireman off."

Ram Singh raced to the door and Wentworth heard his strong voice shouting, heard the rising murmur and cries of terror that answered him. Wentworth whirled and raced to the rear. Nita would stop anyone who attempted to come back from the engine. He, himself, would have to take care of the Pullman conductor, the brakeman, the porters. They would know that he was not an official of the train.

At the door of the first Pullman, he ran into the Pullman conductor with the brakeman at his heels. There was no time to quibble. The Green Fire pressed ever closer, death for them all! Wentworth struck twice quickly. There was a moment of struggle, of outcry, then he laid the two unconscious officials in the smoker. He did not wait to tie them. There was no time! **HE RACED** through the Pullman, shaking berths, crying his warning. "Don't wait to dress!" he shouted. "There isn't time. Get something on your feet and get in the aisles. In a few moments we'll stop the train and everyone must get off. The Pirates, the Pirates that electrocute people, whole trains of people, are going to attack this train! Get ready to get off! Get ready to get off!"

There was a gabble of voices. A woman screamed and a small child bounced out into the aisle, a boy who jumped up and down and clapped his hands in glee. "Oh, goody, goody, *goody!*"

he cried. "I'm going to see some pirates. I'm going to see some pi-i-irates!"

His mother slapped him. Everyone in the car was on the move now. Wentworth raced on to the next, spreading terror with him, deliberately frightening the people into near-panic. Frightening them! There was need for fear, for terror. The Green Fire struck swiftly, struck horribly and once those sputtering jagged points of electric flame darted through the train, there would be none but the dead to see the pirates.

Through car after car he raced on. In the sixth car he saw two men crouched in the shadows. As he entered, they sprang into the light with drawn guns. Wentworth guessed what they were. Government agents on the lookout for the Pirates! They thought they had snared one.

There was no time to argue, no time to convince them of the fearful death that was momentarily speeding toward them with each clicking beat of the wheels upon the rails. Wentworth ducked and plunged toward them. Guns blasted over his head. He slammed his skull into the stomach of one man and nailed him against the side of the narrow passage. His lashing fist caught the second in the jaw and the gun blasted harmlessly a second time. Wentworth whipped out his own revolver then and tapped each on the skull behind the ear, laid them huddled upon the floor and raced on into the next car.

Men and women were standing in frightened postures in the aisles, alarmed by the shots.

"The Pirates!" Wentworth cried. "The Pirates! Get out in the aisles and be ready to get off the train."

Everywhere the cry caused pandemonium, but he stampeded the people, stampeded them into the aisles.

"Stop the train," a woman wailed. "Oh, stop the train."

Wentworth raced on into the last car, got the frightened passengers ready, reached up and yanked the emergency cord. Air hissed in the brakes. They took hold savagely and people stumbled in the aisles. Some fell, others clung to one another in fright. At every platform, Wentworth had thrown wide the doors, raised the covers on the steps so that people could begin piling off the instant the train slowed. They did. Men and women sprawled on the cinder-banked right-of-way in their haste to escape.

Wentworth lashed them from the rear with words, raced through the cars, swinging gymnastically along the rails that held the curtains to get past the congestion of the aisles.

"Hurry, hurry!" he howled. "Death is on the way! Death! The Pirates kill everyone, burn them down with electricity! Like murderers in the death house! Hurry, hurry! Death is on the way!"

Swiftly the cars emptied. Wentworth swung out a doorway and peered ahead. The pilot train of the soldiers had stopped. It was speeding backward toward him! Wentworth cursed. They had caught on more quickly than he had hoped. And they could wreck all his carefully laid plans. He must go on, must race toward the death trap without delay.

Suddenly he threw back his head and laughed. The Spider would find a way. He would save the soldiers' lives, too! Yet there was no time for explanation. Danger threatened on every side. Thousands of lives were at stake in the swift action of the next few seconds. If he failed to get under way, to reach the death trap of the Pirates very close to schedule, they might become suspicious and flee the scene. And thousands of others would perish before again he could set a trap for the killers!

Before he could set a trap! He cursed as he remembered the films Captain Kidd and her giant henchman carried. If he failed tonight, a thousand police and government agents throughout the country would know the Spider's identity, would start a wholesale search for him. How, then, could he hope to trap the Pirates? No, this was his only chance. It must be tonight!

The soldiers' train backed swiftly toward him. He swung back into the coaches, raced ahead. The last persons were straggling out. He yanked open the door of the room where he had put the conductor, carried the unconscious man to a doorway and forced a passenger to carry him to safety. He raced on, found Nita and Jim and Apollo still in the baggage coach.

"Out, darling, fast!" he told Nita.

The girl shook her head. "You must!" Wentworth said sharply. "I'll be safe in the coffin from the Green Fire, but it will take care of only one. You must go!"

Reluctantly, Nita moved with Jim toward the doorway and Wentworth darted on, scrambled up over the coal tender and into the cabin of the locomotive. The pilot train had stopped ahead now, soldiers were spilling out onto the embankment, scores of them. Some were running back at the double toward the halted passenger train, others were deployed to right and left with machine guns and rifles.

"Off, Ram Singh," Wentworth ordered. "Death here. I can protect myself. Not you! Off!"

Ram Singh reluctantly swung to the ground. Wentworth leaned from the window, snatched at the whistle. It wailed like a despairing soul as he jerked the throttle to slow speed. The exhaust blasted, steam hissed, the drivers churned, spraying sparks. Soldiers were in the path of the train, some were struggling to drag ties, heavy logs of wood to the tracks to wreck him.

The Spider yanked the throttle wide!

CHAPTER 20
THE GREEN FIRE

WENTWORTH DRAGGED harder on the throttle, ducked from sight. Lead rattled against the armor plate of the locomotive cabin. He crouched, grim-faced. This was the first time the Spider had ever battled the government of the United States. This was the ultimate defiance! Soldiers with machine guns and rifles bombarded the shelter. A direct hit pinged through the steel, whanged against the opposite side of the cabin.

The Spider defied the government! But it was necessary. There was no time to cavil here, to argue and persuade the men ahead that only the Spider, working alone, could trap the Pirates.

He must run the gauntlet of gunfire, of pelting lead, go on into the death trap of the Pirates alone! There was a shuddering crash as his locomotive slammed into the rear of the empty troop train.

The racing drivers of his locomotive made the mighty giant shudder and tremble, slipping on the rails. Wentworth grabbed the sand lever, dumped grit onto the tracks. There was a shriek as the drivers bit, a jolt, a thundering blast in the exhaust, and the locomotive jolted forward.

The fearful chatter of machine guns blasted now, racking the pounding engine with their leaden hail. A pipe was pierced and geysered steam. A hot water gage smashed. Lead hammered and sprayed and, sometimes, pierced the steel of the locomotive. For moments that seemed hours it continued, then the crash of guns died behind, the shouting and the turmoil of the battle faded.

The soldiers were beaten, but the Spider must act swiftly. He must be within minutes of the spot where the Pirates lurked with their Green Fire. Minutes! And in that time, he must reach the coffin, struggle with it to the cabin of the locomotive, and crawl into it. All this, or his trap for the Pirates would fail!

He sprang to the throttle, set it at half speed, raced back over the avalanching coal and down through the door into the baggage car. He sprinted to its rear, barricaded the door against the possibility that soldiers had clambered into the coaches. Then he whirled to the coffin. He crouched and dragged it up on his back, stumbled forward.

The train lurched sickeningly, rounding a curve, and he heard the clanging of a crossing bell. He had missed a whistle! He thought grimly that the station agent would gape at those empty windows, at those two trains hooked so weirdly together, and dash for his telegraph. Soon the warning would go over the wires. The train might be derailed!

Wentworth cursed as he struggled on with his heavy load. The gap between the baggage car and the coal tender seemed a mile across. He balanced precariously, hunched the coffin forward until he got one end on top the tender. He thrust strongly, sent the ungainly box to security and stepped across, scrambled up the iron ladder.

Almost there now. Ahead he saw a yellow board flash! Good Lord! Were they going to throw a red signal, wreck the train! He cursed savagely, but let the locomotive hammer on. Possibly, they were only trying to stop him. That station agent back there could not have known what had happened. The soldiers could not yet have reached the proper authorities at headquarters to order so drastic a thing as the wrecking of a passenger train!

He dragged the coffin on toward the cabin and let the locomotive thunder on. Hurriedly then, he rigged cord to the throttle so that it and the brake could be jerked from where he lay in the coffin, then he peered out of the window. He was flashing past a red board. He set his teeth. Fighting the government, fighting the railroad, fighting all the world that he might do what all the world had tried in vain to do, to wipe out the Pirates!

He threw himself into the coffin, pulling after him the cords that would control throttle and brakes. He closed the lid, sank back, eyes staring wide at the wood above his head.

PRESENTLY, IF the railroad did not order the train

wrecked, did not spill it in a jumble of fearful wreckage in which he would perish miserably; presently the Green Fire would crackle through every steel inch of this train. But no passengers would die.

He lay waiting and felt the muscles tighten over his body, felt the cold tingle of fear—fear that he might not achieve his end, and fear, too, of the numbing, terrible shock of the Green Fire. Perhaps this coffin was only insulated to resist the electricity if it were placed upon the wooden trestles on which it had lain in the baggage car. Perhaps the steel of the locomotive cabin would throw the Green Fire in upon him!

Wentworth locked his jaws and savagely forced himself to relax, to lie still and wait for the crackling death of the Green Fire. It was not the first time the Spider had lain and waited for possible death, for death in anyone of a dozen terrible forms. But never, he felt, had he waited with such titanic issues hanging upon the result.

God, why didn't they hurry! Every moment now that the blow of the Pirates was delayed, his chances of success were diminished. The soldiers would be acting, flashing messages to headquarters. The train might be turned aside into a ditch. Other corps of soldiers and police might be turned out in towns along the way….

What was that!

Wentworth flung a prayer into the tight air of his coffin, heard the crackling leap of electricity all about, saw the livid glare of the Green Fire sparkle and flash through the narrow opening of his coffin through which ran the cords that would stop the train. He waited until the Green Fire ceased to dance, then he lifted the lid, yanked the cords that snapped on brakes and cut the steam. Then he dropped the lid again.

Just in time. Once more the Green Fire crackled and danced about him. He felt the brakes bite into the wheels, felt the lurch as the locomotive bucked its momentum and slowed. The heat of the dancing fire of death about him penetrated even in the stuffy coffin where he lay rigid. His breath came in gasps and once more the torturing uncertainty of failure rose to confront him. There was such a short distance between the waves of the Green Fire. If the train rolled a few feet too far, crossed the second neutral band and ran between the stiff wires of the third contact of the Green Fire, the third contact that Captain Kidd had mentioned, he would be doomed!

The Green Fire would dance about him without ceasing. He would be unable to escape from the coffin and its outer casing would catch fire. He would be roasted alive, snatched into death on the instant of victory. He held his breath, shuddering with the dread of failure.

The train slowed more and more. It drifted through the second flash of Green Fire and once more the silence, the awful silence of waiting fell over the train. Now, *now*, let the train stop! It must stop now before it rolled against that third set of wires that would loose the Green Fire! Wentworth flung up the coffin lid and stared at the levers. No, there was nothing else he could do. They were set all the way down.

Yes, there was! With a choked cry, he dragged himself from the coffin, leaped at the giant control lever and jerked it into reverse. The huge drive wheels spun and spun, sand grated as Wentworth yanked another lever. The train shuddered, shuddered to a halt and surged backward. He threw the levers into neutral and it stopped. The pilot train ahead surged on. They had not been coupled together. Wentworth's locomotive had been merely pushing the other section and now it raced on. Before it had run ten feet, the Green Fire danced over its steel framework, danced and sparkled in a mocking evil glee.

Wentworth's heart sang. A part of the battle had been won. He need only fight hard and well, risk his life a few more times... He threw back his head in silent laughter. Hope and energy thrilled through him.

The battle was on, a battle against terrific odds! The Pirates were fully a hundred strong, their leader was ruthless and cunning! Yet the Spider laughed! This was his moment! This was his zero hour!

CHAPTER 21
ZERO HOUR

YES, THE zero hour had come! From every shrub along the right of way, from every ravine, men darted toward the train, clambered into its doorways, smashed windows and scrambled through. The looting was on!

Ahead, the flickering Green Fire died out as the pilot train thundered on past the last contact with the current of fearful potency that the Pirates had loosed. Black darkness fell over the scene.

The last of the men was scrambling aboard now and Wentworth heard shouts behind him, shouts of surprise at the empty coaches, shouts of fear that they had been trapped, a bedlam of cries raised to heaven. The Pirates had expected to find corpses they could strip. They found instead, emptiness. It terrified them.

Wentworth peered back along the line of the train, heard their cries. He grinned like a demon, lips thinning back from his teeth. This was the vengeance! With a steady hand, he threw off the brakes, thrust the throttle open. The train creaked and began to roll backward. And ten, fifteen feet, to the rear were the wires that would make it bristle again with the mortal streamers of Green Fire!

Wentworth sprang from the engineer's seat, leaped to the right of way; and rolling, tumbling, springing to his feet, he darted to the underbrush and took cover. Panic was in the coaches now! Men shouted and plunged for the doorways.

Men were dashing for the exits, but there was only a distance of ten feet to roll, ten feet and the train was gaining speed. The drivers spun with the pressure of the steam Wentworth had thrown into the cylinders. Ten feet....

With the abruptness of lightning, the fearful green glow of the Pirates' death fire leaped over the train, leaped and quivered and danced, sparking from coach to coach, quivering in an ecstasy of doom. And within, all was sudden stillness. The lights of the Pirate's torches burned out in the fearful grip of the current. The train went black. The exhaust thundered on and the train rolled, but that was the only sound. The vengeance of the Spider had struck! The Pirates had died in their own trap of fearful death!

But the battle was not yet won. Up there on the hill the leader, that direful woman, Captain Kidd, would be waiting, would be wondering at the recurrence of that fateful fire. But she would not wonder long. She and that giant henchman she called Bolo would flee, race off across the country roads, fleeing the vengeance that had struck their men.

They had millions, those two! They had the weapon of insuperable power. And within a day they could rally a fresh force of fiends to devastate the land, to kill the innocent thousands, to loot and pillage again. They carried, too, the films that would doom the Spider and Nita, that would sweep this last serious obstacle, the Spider, from the path of their savagery!

Wentworth whirled in the underbrush and raced up the hill. Upon that grade there must be a road and somewhere must be parked a thick company of autos in which this horde of Pirates had come to the scene of the kill. As he sprinted, he swept the hillside ahead with his eyes and mid-way up its steep rise, caught the reflection of the Green Fire that sparkled over the train behind, that did its grotesque death dance upon the tops of cars.

That reflection could only come from glass there on the hillside. And glass meant there were autos there. He knew where to strike now. The Spider had his target.

ON WENTWORTH raced up the hillside. The cold glitter of the stars was the only light now, for the train had dragged its last cargo of corpses across the path of the Green Fire and

Captain Kidd fired point-blank at the giant. He wavered

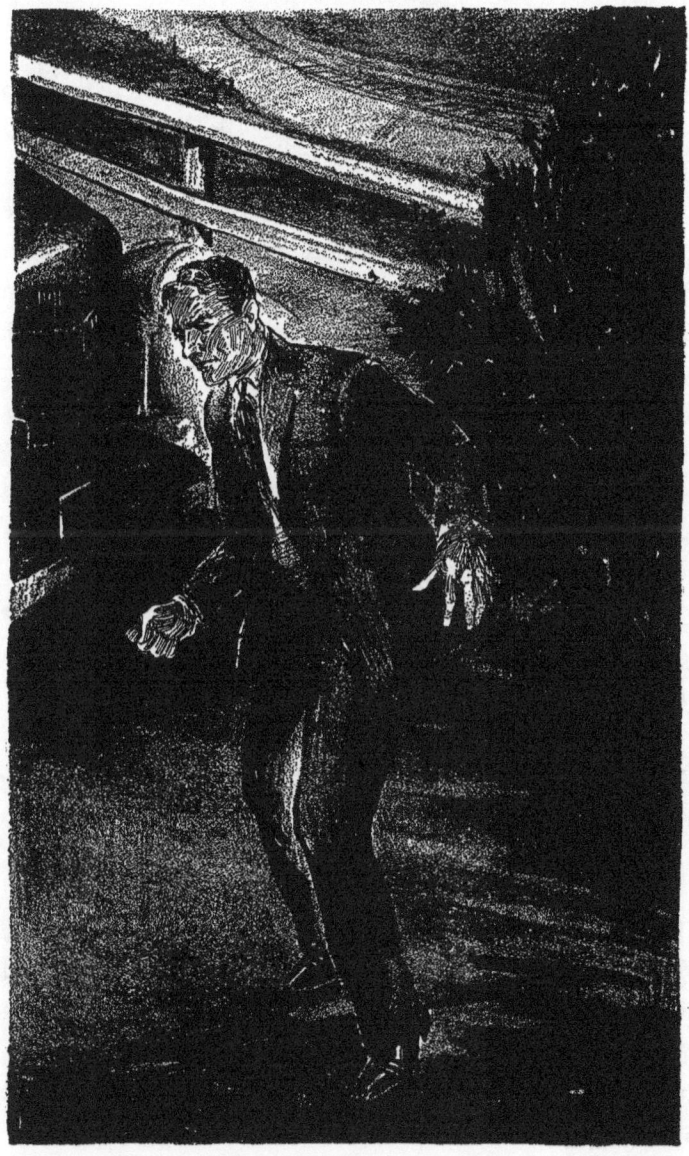

an instant in his stride—then paced on.

its livid flames were dead. By the star's pale distant light, Wentworth made out a break in the trees, a clearing where the auto windows had reflected the Green Fire. There, there he would find the leaders!

He slowed his fierce race and crept forward tensely to the edge of the clearing, peered out past the cars. At first he could make out only the vast gleaming company of cars, fully fifteen or twenty of them, but as he searched rapidly he saw a figure that stiffened him with the rising heat of rage, saw Captain Kidd peering through glasses at the thundering train. She was alone!

A slow, fierce smile twisted Wentworth's mouth. He crouched and, gun in hand, crept almost on hands and knees toward this fearsome leader of the Pirates, toward Captain Kidd!

He was within ten feet of the woman when she snapped the glasses from her eyes and spun toward him. A low cry tore from her throat, but she made no effort to escape. Instead, she snatched at her waist and Wentworth saw that dread knife of hers glitter with the Green Fire of doom. His grim smile fixed on his lips, he straightened and strode toward her.

"Halt!" she said grimly. "Halt! *Or Nita will die!*"

Nita! Wentworth stopped rigidly, staring. The woman had thrust the knife toward the running board of a limousine whose farther side was masked in black shadow. But she had counted without the light from her green glittering knife blade. By its ghastly illumination, Wentworth could see plainly that no one, no woman's form, lay helpless beneath the knife. Captain Kidd was bluffing!

On the point of calling that bluff, of striding forward to strike, he checked himself, listening intently. Yes, there was sound behind him! Footsteps in the underbrush! He allowed consternation to overspread his face, consternation and hopelessness. He let his hands hang so that his automatic dangled useless at his side. He swayed a little on his feet as if inexpressively weary.

"Nita," he moaned, "Nita!"

The woman laughed harshly.

"You are strong," she said, "strong, Spider. But I have beaten you. That's Bolo coming through the woods now."

She stared at the man who stood with drooping shoulders, hanging head before her. The Spider was the image of a beaten man.

She laughed again. "You saved me a lot of trouble, Spider, by killing my men for me. I would have killed them myself in a few moments."

Underbrush crashed directly behind Wentworth now, but he did not whirl to confront this new danger. Instead, he continued to stand with drooping shoulders. This was what he had played for, this was the reason he had feigned despair. He wanted both the major leaders of the Pirates, Bolo and Captain Kidd, before him at one time. He waited for the touch of powerful hands on his shoulders, waited for the moment when the Spider should strike....

Heavily, slowly the footsteps approached. They were within ten feet of him, now five, now.... Wentworth tensed himself for action. Then he realized that the footsteps were not directly behind him, but to one side! He turned his head sluggishly. The bearded Bolo strode even as he himself stood, with heavy shoulders and dangling hands, but there was a difference. Whereas Wentworth's head hung in hopelessness, Bolo's was thrust forward angrily!

THE GIANT strode past Wentworth without once looking his way. He went straight on toward the woman, Captain Kidd, and stalked woodenly forward until he was within five paces of her. The Spider stood unmoving and let him go. Here was a distraction now, the situation he had been playing for. He had the two leaders before him, a gun in his hand. Yet, though the fate of a nation hinged on the deaths of these two, though thousands of lives and millions in wealth demanded their execution, Wentworth stayed his hand. He stood and watched the two confront each other. There was a fierce, throbbing tension in the air. There was death in the set of Bolo's massive shoulders.

He stood now five paces from Captain Kidd.

"So," he said slowly, "you try to kill me, too, try to kill me as you kill that brother of mine, as you kill all the rest!"

"I did not," Captain Kidd denied shortly.

"We made it up to kill the rest, I know," Bolo went on heavily, "but you were to wait until the loot in the mail car had been thrown out. And I was to rob the mail coach. If I hadn't had some trouble entering, I would have been killed like the rest when you turned on the Green Fire."

"I didn't do it," Captain Kidd said swiftly. "It was the Spider. See, there he stands now."

Bolo ignored Wentworth. "I am used to your tricks," he said

heavily. "You wish me to turn my head, then you will shoot. But not me, not me!"

Apparently the man, blind with rage, had not noticed Wentworth! He lifted his clenched fingers before him as if already he grasped the woman's throat, and stalked slowly toward her.

"I have been waiting for this minute," he pronounced gloatingly, "waiting to avenge my brother."

"You're crazy, Bolo," she said. "Get back or I'll shoot you."

"No," said Bolo, still gloatingly, "you tried to kill me with the rest. I kill you now."

Captain Kidd fired point blank at the giant. He wavered an instant in his heavy stride, then paced on, deliberately, unswervingly as fate. Wentworth, his lips smiling grimly, waited….

"You think," Bolo panted, "that your little bullets can stop me? You die, I tell you."

THE WOMAN fired again. Bolo kept on as before, only gusting out breath when the lead smacked into his ribs. His fateful, slow advance drove the woman into a frenzy of fear. She emptied her gun in a mad fusillade of shots that must have torn the heart out of the man. Wentworth stared at the still advancing giant in astonishment. Could any mortal being take five bullets into himself at close range like that and keep on with his grim purpose?

It seemed that Bolo could. He still advanced. Two more steps. The woman was helpless to flee. She shrank away, terrified at the slow fatefulness of his tread.

His arms still stretched before him, his knotted fists still rigid, the fingers working, Bolo took one more stride. Almost within reach of her, he wavered, stumbled and pitched forward as a tree falls. He plunged stiffly, but with his outstretched hands still before him. They caught the woman's skirt and ripped it loose at the waist. She flinched back from those murderous fists, but they seized her ankles and dragged her down.

She fell with a despairing cry! The cry choked off. These hands of fate were upon her throat! But there came then another shout, a shrill frightened cry! Wentworth whirled toward the night-blackened woods beyond this battle of the Titans, saw a thin, angular ghost dart from the darkness, plunge toward the man and woman who struggled on the earth. Good Lord, it couldn't be… but it was! *It was Jonas Curley!*

The aged inventor tottered as he ran. "Don't," he cried in a broken voice. "Don't! In God's name, if you must kill, kill me!"

He hurled himself upon the pair. But already Bolo's great form had stiffened, his fingers death locked about the woman's throat.

"Ah, don't," he begged, and now his breath was sobbing. "Forgive her. I forgive. If I can, surely you… Ah, kill me. I do not want to live!"

But neither Bolo nor Captain Kidd made answer. Together in life—they had gone together into death….

WENTWORTH STARED at Jonas Curley a moment, then nodded. Many things were clear now. He knew now why Captain Kidd had gone into that long explanation of why she had killed Nellie Curley and Dutch Brogard. She had been justifying to herself the murder of her niece.

"Of course," he said to Curley, "it had to be your daughter, the blonde girl I saw in your rooms the two times I was there." He strode closer, looked down at the woman. He had seen Curley's daughter, Joan, twice before, it was true. But each time there had been something to prevent his seeing her clearly enough to identify her as Captain Kidd.

The first time, she had only peered over her father's shoulder and the light had been behind her. The face had been in black shadow. The second time the light had been dim, too, and she had pretended tears. She had kept a handkerchief before her face throughout the conversation. Her hair undoubtedly had been blonde. She had cut it short and dyed it black to prevent identification and thereafter she had worn a blonde wig at home. The only thing he had seen clearly on his two visits to the home was that the daughter had blonde hair....

Wentworth spoke softly to Curley, almost as if he were talking to himself.

"I knew it must be some one in the family," he told the aged inventor. "I realized it must be some one close to you when your life was spared after you were taken captive. Then, too, you killed those two men who might have betrayed your daughter."

A hand touched Wentworth's arm and he flinched away, whirling to battle, then caught himself in mid-blow. It was Nita!

"I tried to get here in time, Dick," she said swiftly. "I held up an auto with a gun and—"

She stopped, gripping Wentworth's arms with both hands and stared at the two bodies on the ground, at the aged inventor. Tears glistened on Curley's cheeks.

189

"Captain Kidd," the old man said sadly, "why did you do it, child? Why did you do it?" He picked up the dead body in his arms and rocked it tenderly as a baby. "I used to call you Captain Kidd, little girl, and you used the name to mock me. You corrupted my granddaughter and made her turn against me. You killed my grandson. You shouldn't have done that. Listen, child, why did you do that?"

"He's mad," Nita whispered.

Wentworth jerked his head quickly, walked over to Jonas Curley and put his hand on the old, bent shoulders. "Would it help you to know, Mr. Curley, that your granddaughter was true to you? That she was killed because she would not help these criminals?"

Slowly the old man's head came up. He stared up into Wentworth's face.

"You wouldn't fool an old man?" he pleaded. A wildness of hope, of incredible hope, was in his voice. The memory of that scene in the mountains, of his mourning for his lost "little Nell" came back to Wentworth. But he knew how incredibly the man loved his granddaughter. Wentworth could understand love....

"I wouldn't fool you," Wentworth said slowly. "Your granddaughter was true to you. That was why she was killed."

"Nellie!" the old man cried. "Nellie!"

He jerked to his feet like a man made of brittle sticks. He seized Wentworth by the shoulder. "You wouldn't lie to me," he said hoarsely, with pitiful hope. "If Nellie, if only Nellie—"

"She was true to you to the end," Wentworth said positively.

Jonas Curley raised his stiff old arms to heaven. "Oh, thank God, thank God!" he cried.

He looked down at his daughter as if he did not see her, then raised his hands to heaven again in silent prayer, and the wet tracery of tears glistened on his cheeks. His arms fell. His head sagged. He stumbled off into the night.

Wentworth watched him go, then he stared down at the bodies on the ground. He knelt by them swiftly and his search was rewarded. He straightened with rolls of films in his hands, the films of the Spider making his kill. Swiftly he unreeled them and set them afire, scattered the fragile ashes over the earth. The Spider could battle on now. The world had been saved from these fiends....

He flopped the giant Bolo over on his back and, dipping a finger in the man's blood, he traced a crude design of the Spider upon his forehead and upon that of the woman. For once, the Spider had no seal to imprint!

He turned then to Nita. "Come, darling. The soldiers will be here any moment now. We must be gone."

"But Jonas Curley?" she queried, looking up into his face.

Wentworth shook his head slowly. "He will be all right, I think, with the memory of his granddaughter to bolster him, the assurance that she played fair with him."

Nita said, "But, Dick, she wasn't true to him. They killed her because they knew police were on her trail and thought they might be discovered through her. The flag was just savagery. Dick, you lied to old Jonas."

Wentworth squeezed Nita's shoulders. "Of course I lied,

darling," he said quietly. "Jonas Curley already has too much sorrow for anyone human being to bear. A white lie is a small price to pay—if it will bring about even a slight lessening of the load of suffering on his old shoulders."

As he spoke, Wentworth was guiding Nita toward the edge of the clearing—and the safety which lay in flight.